RETICENT

A Somber Soul in Despair

(RASSID)

ANTWON LINDSEY

RETICENT
A Somber Soul in Despair

www.AntwonLindsey.com

Library of Congress Control Number: 20107909597

ISBN-13: 978-1547092758
ISBN-10: 1547092750

Printed in the United States

CONTENTS

This novel is respectfully dedicated to my son Ayden and the hopeful youth, who will liberate our world into one of peace & social equality.

Sincerely,

Yours Truly

RASSID: Spotify Playlist

Writing this book, I saw each chapter as a scene within a film, so I created a playlist to help readers capture the essence & ambience of the characters' emotional path within each chapter. To listen to the playlist, login to Spotify and search:

RASSID Playlist

I

Preface

THEY SAY that life for a young Black American male being raised in Urban America can only go one of three ways: You either take your butt off to college to get out the hood, spend the rest of your life behind bars in a maximum security prison because you thought that living the street life was the move, or you end up at the coroner's office; laying lifeless on a table all over some beef you got into with a guy you used to kick it with way back in middle school. I tell you - growing up in the hood there ain't no love, there ain't no care and it most definitely ain't no hope lingering around here anywhere. People are broke and can't get a job; yet, they'll do anything to make sure that they're stunting on the next person. Even if that means riding in that newest BMW but don't have a pot to piss in, lights on at home, or even food in the fridge to eat.

That's because - in the hood - don't anybody give a crap about how you feel on the inside. It's all about how good you look on the outside. From the name brand clothes and shoes. To the expensive bundles of hair weaves and makeup kits.

The thing that's messed up about it all is not that people in the hood are oblivious to the problems that plague our communities. The reality of it all is that we have become complacent to the mistreatment, social inequality, and seamlessly accepted the negative stigmas that have been branded upon our communities. All of which have become thoroughly cemented into the very fabric of our communities, as a result of the constant misguided narratives from mainstream media via; news outlets, television shows and Hollywood films that continue to devalue black culture.

With constant media coverage of every shooting, robbery, and anything else that promotes a destructive story of Black America. Now, let's not get started on the self-invested politicians that thrive on creating culturally biased policies or even the conglomerate corporations that spend most of their time exploiting the culturally vibrant inner-city communities, who aren't doing anything but adding more fuel to this undesirable flame of self-destruction.

It's crazy how things are so messed up in the hood that most people don't even realize that our communities are gradually being snipped away from us: one house and small business at a time through this strategic process of gentrification. The connected are buying up the property, astronomically raising the cost of living, which inevitably leads to the displacement of black families and the closing of black-owned businesses. In displacing families and cultures, the gentrifiers must also displace the pathologies that have kept the communities downtrodden and deprived of so many resources.

How I see it, Black Americans are persistently fighting two wars. One that involves trying to maintain a valued and sustainable living for themselves but eventually progresses into them becoming slaves to commercial labor. Devoting more hours at work instead of exploring their talents and gifts. Barely spending the necessary time at home nurturing their young and impressionable children.

In most urban communities, many young Black Americans fail to get the proper educational training due to a lack of funding for inner-city schools, as well as, minimal parental involvement or guidance along their educational pathways. This lack of training leaves them to desire only one other option: to go out and 'get it by any means' as it would be said.

The other war we simultaneously undergo encompasses the impacts of many undiagnosed mental health disorders because of "suppressing" the extensive amount of bull we must go through as Black Americans living in Urban America. Attempting to survive in an environment that continues to stagger the enrichment of our youth and their immediate success.

As Baldwin is often quoted, "To be a Negro in this country and to be relatively conscious is to be in a rage almost all the time."

Every day we are forced to stay active, fighting back the restless desire to shed tears as loved ones are killed in senseless acts of violence. We struggle with the constraints of being raised in an environment of emotional neglect compounded by the animosity and venom from those nearby who have never realized their hopes and dreams.

The crushing, yet the unacknowledged weight of not seeing value in seeking your true potential because the world has convinced you to be "okay" with less and that you aren't "good" enough anyway. Forces you to take shelter in an empty closet of isolated regret. Having no real role models to guide you towards the light of success or anyone to express your deepest thoughts. Growing hopeless of ever finding someone, who will be keen to listening and understanding the hurt resting upon your heart.

At times, it would seem as if the world around you can care less about your existence. So you often wish you weren't alive and to escape it all you roll up them potent California trees, drink away your sorrows with a cup of dark liquor, place your middle fingers high in the sky, while saying to the rest of the world "kiss my ass," as the painful memories of your life temporarily fade away.

Left on your own to drown the sounds in your head, that continuously play the same old tune of misery and a self-perpetuated regret that you've gained for your very own existence. It is too often as Black people that we fail to acknowledge the emotional trauma of one's life to being a serious matter worthy of our concerns. Study after study has shown that living in poverty leaves mental scars and PTSD, like war and other major traumatic events.

Society blames us for our problems, and we find it just as convenient to blame society for the problems we face. We need to get beyond the toxic masculinity of crushing and suppressing our emotions by admitting that on the inside - we long to receive understanding from our peers and families. Yearning to feel the sensational excitement of being appreciated for our divine presence. Society should recognize that if a person can be acquitted of DUI, vehicular manslaughter, and other crimes due to "AFFLUENZA"; then poverty is much more deserving of recognition for factors in the lives of those trapped in its ever-gaping maw.

In casting these stones of hypocrisy, we often riot when a cop kills a black woman or male because of their alleged threat based on of his/her physical appearance; but encourage acts of revenge when something immoral has been done to a family member by other blacks of our community. Taking literally the interpretation of, "An eye for an eye."

As a whole, we must consider, "what is it that we are willing to sacrifice for the better making of youth within minority communities, as well as, how do we efficiently enrich our youth that is limited by resource availability?"

CHAPTER 1

Sore Roots

IT WAS 1997, almost seven months since Tupac passed away and left the world staggered in disbelief. My pops was a hardworking man employed by the City of Miami Solid Waste Department. Some say he reminded them of that one rapper named "Common Sense" because of his smooth demeanor, butter pecan complexion and how he'd always rock a clean bald head. He was just clocking at work around 2:00 pm, when one of his co-workers yelled out to him, "Aye Yo, D!" They called my pops "D" as a nickname, but his government name was Derrick Mills. Pops calmly yelled back, "Yo! What's Up?" A guy wearing a blue uniform jumpsuit with dirty black work boots walked over from the other side of the room to dap pops up, when he paused and said, "Aye, D. I got to go out to my daughter school tomorrow man. She having a lil school performance tomorrow night and I'm supposed to be there by 6:30 pm. You think you can cover my overnight for me big dawg? I know you need the hour's man, so that's why I came to ask you."

As understanding as he was, Pops said to him jokingly, "Yeah man, you know I got you. But what makes you think I need the hours anyway?" The guy replied sarcastically, "Bruh! How else you think I know? Didn't you just have a baby not too long ago? I know you gon' need some extra chips for them pampers and baby formula. I figured I'd ask you instead of these other chumps. Plus, I knew I could count on you since you owed me from the times I had to cover yo ass when you needed to go to them doctors' appointments with yo crazy ass baby mama."

"Aye, watch yo mouth bout my son moms," Pops said with a smirk on his face, "But you right though. You did come through for me when I needed you. I can't argue with that. What your baby girl performing tomorrow?" he asked the guy. "Man shoot, I don't even know. I think they're doing Romeo and Juliet or something like that. To be honest, when her mama calls me and tells me stuff like this - I don't even be trying to go into detail about it. You know how she is man. Every time we get on the damn phone, she starts bringing up stuff that ain't got nothing to do with our daughter. Yesterday she going to tell me, 'I dare you not to show up because I'm waiting to call the child support people on your ass.'

"This girl always out here threatening to call the child support people on me as if I don't already pay child support. Man, I'm telling you she crazy. Then how about she gon' try and tell me that, 'I don't pay enough.' Talking about that's not even sufficient to buy her school clothes and help pay the rent.

"Yo, I done showed you my check. Those people take four hundred and eighty dollars out of my check every pay period. So I told her money hungry ass, 'First of all I ain't yo man, so I ain't got to be paying yo rent and maybe if you quit spending seventy-five dollars to get your nails done every other week or stop using the child support money to buy your weave, then maybe you'll have some money to pay your own damn rent.'

"Boy I tell you, sometimes I wish I never even met that girl man, she be pissing me off. So, what I'ma do is – I'ma just show up at this lil performance tomorrow and when it's over - I'ma clear it. This way I ain't got to hear her loud mouth talking about I don't do nothing for my daughter or never show support."

Pops stood there listening, as he laughed before saying, "Man you a fool. You know you still want her dawg cause if you didn't, you wouldn't be arguing with her all the time." The guy responded dramatically, "Man stop playing. Trust me; I wouldn't get back with her ass if the world was ending and we were the last two people on earth - you tripping."

"Yeah aight, that's what you say, but I bet you still

sliding on her though," Pops said to him with a big grin. His co-worker started to laugh and was like "Haha man you wild, I do – but I mean - not all the time though. Just now and then, you know - only when she ain't tripping on me about dumb stuff."

"See that's your problem right there. You don't want to leave that girl alone man. You'd lose your mind if you did. You done trapped yourself boy but aye man I can't judge you," Pops told him. "But for real though, you just make sure you show up for your lil girl and don't be out here playing with her feelings because you can't get things situated with her mama."

The guy laughed as he reached in to dap my pops up again. "Ha-ha you crazy," he said. "I'm always going to be there for my baby girl no matter what. But aye, I appreciate you though man. You always keep it real but listen; I'm about to go ahead and get ready to hop on these folk's truck. They got me working in Overtown today, so I'll holla at ya' later player."

"Aight then playa," Pops replied as he reached in for the dap "I'll holla at you later; You be easy, be safe."

My aunty Shay said that back in the day, the old boy was a cool and soulful dude. A humble guy that loved his job, he enjoyed hanging out with the fellas from time to time, but most of all he savored the precious moments that he would spend with me. She told me when he would come over to the house, as soon as, he would step foot through the door I'd come crawling right up to him drooling in excitement. He'd pick me up in his arms, toss me in the air, and kiss my forehead before telling me how special I was to him. By this time, he and the old girl had already split up shortly after I was born.

As the story goes, while Pops was out busting his butt to put food on the table every day, the old girl had other plans in mind. She was a few years younger than him when they met, so her mind was still quite immature. While the old man would be gone off to work, she'd be out partying, spending his money and fooling around with some fake gangster dude that claimed he ran the streets.

I heard that when she was young, her dad was one of the top dope dealers before he passed away from a heroin overdose. So, it's no surprise that she would be attracted to a dude that went hard in the streets because it was all she ever knew; it probably reminded her of my granddaddy. But when Pops got word that his girl was out there in the streets wildn', he denied the claims at first, but after becoming increasingly agitated with folks always bringing it up, he decided to ask my mom about it.

One weekend when he didn't have to go in for work, he wanted to do something spontaneous and surprise my mom by taking her out somewhere nice. It was a warm night in Miami; the street lights glimmered like candles in the evening sky as they pulled up to the moderately upscale restaurant called Shantel's.

Just a few blocks away from the Dolphins stadium and the equivalent of any restaurant you'd find in South

Beach, Miami. Many Blacks came here to eat because of its outstanding quality of soul food dishes. The place was packed and full to the brim with hungry families and couples dressed in their finest evening wear.

The moment they stepped into the restaurant, the old girl began acting impolite and excessively sassy towards Pops. She started complaining, questioning his reasoning for bringing her there, said the food looked nasty and kept talking about how bored she was starting to get once they were seated. Genuinely confused by this, pop went ahead and called for the check so that he could take her home because maybe she'd be ready for what he had planned for her next.

As they drove home, the tension continued to rise when she purposely ignored him as he struggled to start up a conversation. Distancing herself, she turned her back to him and scooted so far to the right in the passenger seat that her body was pasted against the door as she gazed outside of the window.

Pops gently reached over in concern, to see what was wrong but immediately she forcefully shoved his hand away from the bare skin of her smooth thigh, rudely commanding him to "STOP!"

From that point, the rest of the car ride home was filled with the sound of wind seeping through the cracks of the car window, as the streetlights above, flashed through the droplets of water dripping down the windshield.

They pulled up to the driveway of pop's small two bedrooms, one bathroom duplex but as he switched the key to turn the car off, moms slammed the passenger door shut and headed towards the front door of the duplex. Watching her walk away in an undiagnosed fast-pace of fury, Pops slowly shook his head, while releasing a deep sigh of confusion. Usually, she'd wait for pops to open the door for her, but this was unusual, so it left the old man wondering, "What was up with her tonight?"

Trying to comprehend what was putting mom in such a bad mood, he attempted to affectionately hug her from behind as she got undressed in the bedroom. But, to his disappointment, she shrugged him away in disgust.

"Yo, Bri," He said to my mom, "What's going on with you babe? I have been trying to talk to you all night, but you ain't said a word to me since we left the restaurant and every time I try to touch you, you keep acting funny with me. What's going on? Did I do something wrong? Just let me know something because I'm legit confused right now and don't understand why you are acting like this towards me." Still undressing, she completely ignored his search for an answer before brushing against his shoulder to head into the bathroom.

As she strutted out of the bedroom, pop stood there in complete dismay, while placing his right hand over his face, closing his eyes and taking a deep breath, attempting to get a grip on his is apparent frustration with her. Sitting down on the bed, he kicked off his shoes and began to get undressed so that he could meet moms in the bathroom to see if he would be able to solve this problem amid a beautiful and steamy shower.

Approaching the bathroom door, excited about his method of fixing things, pops joy was short lived when he twisted the doorknob and felt that the door was locked. Looking down at the crack beneath the door, he could see the flickering of a candle as the sound of running water from the shower head collided with the bathtub.

Sensing that this might have meant she probably needed some space, he backed away from the door, strolled to the living room and waited until she was done using the bathroom. Sitting on the leather sofa allowing his mind to wander, all of the possible reasons as to why she might be acting weird towards him ran through his brain. But one thought out of all others seemed to grow uncomfortably dominant to him. It was the one he'd been trying to avoid for months, but with the way things had been going tonight, he questioned the possibility of it being true.

Wrapped in a red towel, a cloud of steam rushed from the bathroom as the door swung open. Moms exited the bathroom and leisurely made her way down the dim hallway towards the bedroom. Glancing over his shoulder at her, Pops immediately became overwhelmed with the idea of the possibility that she could be cheating on him.

With her spending over an hour in the shower, he knew she had used most of the hot water, which meant that he'd have to wait another thirty minutes before using it himself if he didn't want to take a cold shower. It also meant that he had now gained an extra thirty minutes to butter her up and try to get her to talk to him.

Plodding down the hallway to the bedroom shortly after, Pops was on a mission to get mom to talk because this ignoring stuff wasn't working out for him. At the bedroom door, he jiggled the knob to enter, but again found himself faced with another locked door. So, to be slick and have her open the door, Pops yelled out, "Bri, can you pass me a pair of clean underwear? I forgot to take them out of the drawer."

After a few seconds passed of him waiting patiently, she still hadn't opened the door causing him to grow even more irritated with her childish behavior. "I'm not about to play these games with her," he said to himself before walking into the kitchen to find a knife.

Scavenging through a kitchen drawer of silverware, he eventually found a butter knife that he could use to slide past the door hinge. He firmly held onto the doorknob with his left hand while jimmying the lock with the butter knife in his right hand, and in less than thirty seconds a small "CLINK" sounded off as the door cracked open.

Slowly widening the door with the push of his left hand, in a brief state of mental paralysis, he stood in the doorway baffled by what he was witnessing in front of him. Stunned and completely uncertain of what was going on at this point he entered the room in complete confusion.

"Bri! Babe, what's going on? You packing up, what you packing up for? Whatever I did, trust me I'm sorry. Just let me fix it, but first you got to talk to me and tell me what I did wrong, for me to do that," he whimpered, as he entered the bedroom. Noticeably unbothered by his plea, she continued to ignore him as she gathered her belongings.

"Listen, I don't get what's going on. First, you hate the fact I tried to take you out for a nice dinner, then you distanced yourself, ignoring me the whole ride back home not even allowing me to touch you and now you're in here packing up your stuff? This is some bullshit Bri, can you at least just tell me what's on your mind? It doesn't have to be like this; I'm sure we can talk this crap out, whatever it is."

Still, moms continued to plead the fifth as she pulled her clothes out of the drawers, took her perfumes off the top of the dresser and packed everything into the big Coach duffle bag, Pops had bought her for Valentine's Day earlier this year.

It was eating him up on the inside, causing him to feels as though dozens of ants were starting to crawl all over his body, while his heart began to sink into a cold and shallow abyss. Anxiously trying to gain insight on what might have caused this situation to occur, he remained startled because he had never seen this one coming.

"So, you not at least going to attempt to explain to me what's going on? You're just going to pack up your stuff and bounce, just like that? This is crazy; I swear I can't even believe you right now, yo. All the things I've done for you and this is how you repay me by ignoring me and then leaving me. Man, I swear you just about the most selfish person I have ever met in my life," he said to her.

"Boy!" She said, before a great pause – "Ugh, would you just shut the hell up. You always talking about what you've done for somebody when you ain't do shit for me that I couldn't do for myself. I swear yo ass make me sick sometimes, damn. You sound worse than a female sitting over here complaining about shit you supposed to do. Just leave me alone and stop talking. Go somewhere else, cause you getting on my last nerve right now."

"Man what?" Pops said in an aggressive tone. "I ain't trying to argue, but you need to watch who the hell you think you talking to? You ain't about to just speak to me no any kind of way; you got me messed up. I ain't one these other cats you been out here in the streets messing with. Yeah, you think I ain't know but Scooter them was telling me all about you and how you out here doing dirt sliding on these other dudes while I'm at work. I didn't want to believe 'em at first, but you just proved them right."

"Boy, whatever," she replied. "You can believe whatever the hell you want to believe cause don't nobody know shit about me and what I do. So like I said, go on somewhere before I hurt yo feelings," moms said back to him in a cold, threatening way.

"Trick you can't hurt my feelings. You know what - as a matter of fact, hurry up and pack your stuff so you can get the hell up out of my damn house. I'm done playing these games with you! Every time I try to do something good for you, you end up finding some way to ruin it or throw some bull in my face. Hurry and grab yo stuff man; I'm through with this bullshit you got going."

"Whatever, I can care less about what you are saying cause its fine with me, sweetie. Trust me, honey, you don't have to tell me twice. Ugh, I swear I can't stand you! You just about the dumbest person I ever met in my life. Talking like I need you. Boy, don't nobody need your ass. You can't do anything for me. You can't even afford to take care of your damn self, still wearing the same ass old clothes you had from five years ago. No, you got me messed up if you thought I was gone be with your old bum ass forever. Boy please," moms replied.

Pops' blood instantly began to boil like a pot full of boiled peanuts. His fist clenched, and the inside of his soul quivered as he thought to himself on how bad he wanted to punch her lights out but knew he couldn't do that because she was a female and still his baby's mom. He remained frozen in disbelief.

Mumbling to herself, she continued with saying, "Ass ain't never around no way. Don't even have enough time to be with your own family, always talking about you got to go to damn work or do some over time. Hell, yo ass should be happy I ain't get pregnant by somebody else."

By the time she finished packing her stuff, pops had already left the bedroom to avoid making matter worse.

That's when the old girl called out to him from the dark hallway, "Uhm - I'm done now so you can take me home."

Snapping out his daze of regret and heartache pops replied, "Take you home? Man, you better call a cab or tell whatever dude you been messing with to come pick you up."

"Uhm, excuse me! You brought me over here; then you can take me back where I came from. I'm not about to call a Society cab or walk. So, get your ass up and let's go so you can take me back home to my son."

Pops hated when she said, "my son" as if he had nothing to do with my birth. But being the good dude he was, Pops kissed his teeth, snatched his car keys off the living room table and headed for the front door slamming the door so hard it mimicked the sound of a lightning storm.

It was a sobering moment for Pops because he knew this was the end for real this time. Occasionally they'd argue about little petty stuff but would make up with each other almost immediately after they had come to their senses. But now – this one was on another level. This time it was official, and he just knew that they wouldn't be able to bounce back from it all.

After nearly driving thirty miles over the 45mph city speed limit, they arrived at my grandma's place where my mom lived. It was around 11:00 pm, so people were still hanging outside drinking alcohol, having conversations while the faint sound of the Notorious B.I.G.s song 'One More Chance' played from someone's car nearby.

Angrily pushing forward the seat of his two-door car, she pulled her bags from the back and made her way up the apartment complex. Sitting in the driver's seat with his hand propped on his head, Pops decided he'd at least get out the car to see me while he was here.

Walking up to the shadowed stairway, he had to maneuver through a group of nosey tenants that were perched at the bottom of the staircase. He knocked on the door. "Who is it?" Someone responded from inside of the house. "It's Derrick," he replied.

The door slowly opened, and it was my aunty. "Oh - Hey Derrick, you alright? You know she came in here being all extra talking about, y'all got into a fight and what not; so you might not want to bother her right now."

My aunty Shay was cool, she knew how their relationship went and knew that my dad was a good dude who barely raised his voice, even if he was ordering food at the drive-thru of a fast-food restaurant.

"Naw, Shay it ain't even like that. I just came up to see to see the baby really quick," he said to her, as he spotted me on the floor laying down peacefully in a makeshift bed. My aunty was in the living room watching TV as she babysat me, so she had laid me down on a pallet on the floor so I wouldn't roll off the couch.

"Okay," she said. "I was just checking; you know

you my dawg." Pops smiled and replied, "Ha-ha – that's why I mess with you Shay you already know what's real," as he hugged her before entering the apartment to greet me.

As I was sleeping peacefully on my pallet, Pops kneeled and slowly picked me up careful enough to not wake me. "Awe - look at Daddy's big boy," he said while staring at me as I now laid slumped across his right shoulder. He paced back and forth for a few moments before sitting down at the small dining room table holding me in his arms.

Smiling as bright as the sun, he gently whispered– "Aye Shay, you know this my boy, right? This my main man right here. He going to be a smart lil dude when he gets older," is all he could muster out before moms came busting out through her bedroom door.

"WHAT THE HELL ARE YOU DOING IN MY HOUSE?" she yelled out.

Still holding me in his arms, Pops got up and started to head towards the door, so he could sit outside on the porch with me for a few minutes. Not aware of his plans, moms raced over to him, pushed him sideways and tried to snatch me out of his arms.

"Yo, what the hell is your problem?" The old boy responded angrily. "You ain't finna go nowhere with my baby, I don't know who the hell you think you are, but you better put my baby down," she said fiercely.

"Man ain't nobody worried about you, go sit your

ass down somewhere before you wake the baby up. Who the hell you talking to?" she said to him, while forcefully pressing her finger against pops face.

He stumbled back into the front door as he attempted to avoid her hand from swiping at his face. "Bri, you need to chill out, now is not the time. Just go on about your business," the old man replied while restraining his thoughts of kicking her in the chest. She had now woken me up with her shenanigans, so my pops began to pat me on the back saying, "It's okay baby - go back to sleep baby, go back to sleep."

My aunty stood up from the couch and said, "Derrick just give me the baby and leave." Pops responded, "Naw Shay, she be tripping. She can't stop me from spending time with our son; you got to be out of your mind. We are going on this porch and she going to leave me alone, that's what she going to do."

"Oh, so now all of a sudden y'all two just as cool as ever huh? Y'all must be doing each other the way y'all be acting," moms said to them in a nasty tone.

"Girl now you know damn well, I ain't got nothing going on with Derrick. I ain't you; I know how to keep a man when I have one. Go head Derrick - take him outside for a lil bit, you right. I don't know what her problem is but she done chose the right one."

"Preciate you Shay," Pops replied in relief. But my mom wasn't backing down. "Trick, who the hell do you think you are? Gon' tell somebody they can go outside with my baby. Trick you must've lost your damn mind. You know what - don't worry, I got a treat for that ass." She then turned around and marched over to the telephone near the kitchen entrance.

"Hello! Yes, excuse me, but I want to report a kidnapping. My son's father just came over to my apartment and is trying to leave with him without my permission. He said he going to kill everybody in the house if I don't hang up the phone," my mom said to a 9-1-1 operator.

Looking at her in complete disappointment, my aunty turned around, peeped her head out of the door to warn my dad that the police might be coming. "Derrick you better leave brother, she just called the cops on you lying talking about you're trying to kidnap the baby and that you gon' kill everybody. Let me get him so you can leave."

"Man, naw Shay, she on some real bull right now and I ain't got time for it. I ain't going nowhere, I'ma sit right here on these steps with my son and if the police got something to say about it then they just gon' have to say it. She tripping, like for real though Shay."

Instead of keeping it real with the old boy from the get, moms found any reason to point the finger at him. When the cops came, she tried to convince them that he was going to harm me. Aunty didn't say much when the cops asked her what happened because it wasn't her business, but she began to despise my mom for what she was doing to my pops.

By now the entire neighborhood was up being nosey and waiting to see what was going on so that they could have something to run they mouths about the next day. Pops eventually talked to one of the officer's one on one and let them know what had happened that night, so he didn't go to jail. But since the old girl was petty she put a restraining order on pops that wouldn't allow him to come within five hundred feet of her. It meant that he couldn't come over to visit me.

The next day she went downtown and opened a child support case that wouldn't allow him to see me until things were finalized. But my pops, being the ripe guy, he was, he didn't let it get the best of him. I'm sure on the inside it ate him alive to not be able to spend time with me, heck he probably even cried about it at some point, but still, he didn't let that stop him from loving me.

When my aunty would have to babysit me, she'd let him know whenever she'd be going to the Flea Market on 79th street and he'd leave work early just to see me. Pops even gave my aunty extra money for the both of us because he knew she understood how deeply he cared for me and how much he wanted me to be there with him. But in April of 97', everything would soon change.

It was the next day of work for my pops, the same day he had promised his co-worker that he'd take on his late-night shift. Tired and ready to head home from a long day of work, Pops clocked out of work around eight minutes past midnight after working a near twelve-hour shift. Walking sluggishly to his car, he yawned widely before he cranked up the engine to the car to leave the job parking lot.

Cruising through the quietly vibrant Liberty City streets, my pops was heading west on 46th Street & 27th Avenue when he approached a red light. Yawning and trying to keep himself awake, he turned off the a/c in his 1983 Cutlass Supreme, rolled the windows down and slowly turned up the Tupac 'So Many Tears' track that was playing as he came to a slow stop.

Waiting at the light, he tilted his head down to awkwardly peep up and catch a glimpse of the last southbound Metrorail train passing by above. The light was long as heck, so he said, "Bump that," and decided that he'd just put the car in neutral. His forearm swung outside of the window as he attempted to catch the dry breeze of the night. When suddenly, in his rear-view mirror he saw a tall black figure walking on the left side of the street.

Quickly he turned around to see what the person looked like but a large tree in front of a nearby house cast a huge shadow on the sidewalk making it hard to see anything. Being street smart, Pops sensed that something wasn't right, so he hurried to crack open his glove compartment and reached for his pistol.

Always keeping one bullet in the head was the rule of the street, so pulling his gun out he waited anxiously in preparation for whatever was about to happen next.

Continuously checking in his side and rear-view mirror, Pops could see that the person was now crossing over into the street towards the car.

In a rush, he scooted himself upright in the seat, making sure he clutched onto his pistol tightly. This way if anything popped off he'd be ready to start busting at whoever was attempting to rob him. He didn't want to be out here and get caught slipping tonight. His body began to get that warm feeling of adrenaline, as the tension rushed through his veins. His stomach grew shallow with fear as he thought to himself, "Why me, man? I ain't trying to shoot nobody."

Pops heart began racing as the ghostly silhouette of what appeared to be a man started to get alarmingly close to the car. Watching carefully, Pops turned sideways and slid the gun towards the middle of his lap. He never needed to use his gun except for a few times at the gun range, but this was an entirely different circumstance. At this period of night in the city, there was no telling of what could go down this late.

Then suddenly it happened. The guy was at the car door, and before you knew it Pops pulled up his pistol and said with a demanding tone, "What's Up!"

Swiftly raising his hands and slightly turning his head away to the left, in a soft, scratchy voice the man cried out, "Don't shoot, don't shoot. Please, sir, Please!"

Staring at the terrified dirty face, bushy beard,

dreaded hair and smelling the odor of a man who seems as if he hasn't taken a shower in months. Pop's pounding heart slowly came to ease but remained skeptical of his surroundings and the person that was now standing outside of his car door.

"I only wanted to know if you had some spare change, that's all. Please don't shoot," the homeless guy pleaded. Sensing that there wasn't any real threat to his life pops slowly began to lower his gun, as he scouted the rest of the street in case this might have been a setup.

"Man, what the hell are you doing walking up on somebody this late at night, I could've shot yo ass man," he told the guy. "You lucky I wasn't one these crazy ass dudes out here with nothing to lose or else I probably would've killed yo ass – for no reason."

"Sorry sir," the man replied in a vulnerable voice, "I just thought I'd ask you for some spare change that's all. I just wanted some to see if you had some spare change he repeated."

"Yeah! Yeah! Yeah! Hold up," Pops said in an agitated manner as he reached over and started to ruffle through the ashtray in his car where he kept all of his change. "Thank you, thank you. God, bless you," the homeless man said to pops.

Continuing to search for the quarters, Pops could see that the light going northbound had just turned yellow which meant that his light going west was getting ready to turn green at any moment. Not wanting to get stuck at the long ass light again, he yanked out the entire ashtray and dumped all the change into the man hands.

The coins went flying as some of them fell onto the ground leading the homeless guy to say to pops, "Don't worry about it, I got it. Thank you so much, God bless you, sir," as he kneeled down to pick up the rest of the change.

With the light now green, Pops switched the gear into drive and yelled out to the pale man "Aight now, you be safe out here and stop running up on people cars before you get shot," as he slowly pulled off.

Being preoccupied with the homeless guy, Pops didn't see that there was an eighteen-wheeler semi-truck speeding north up the avenue in a last-minute attempt to beat the red light. So, as soon as pops pulled out to head across the intersection, without warning all you could hear was the loud screeching of tires and then a thunderous crack that shook the entire neighborhood.

The semi had slammed right into pops car sending him tumbling down the street until it landed upside down slightly spinning. Some folks a few blocks down were hanging outside drinking and listening to music in front of their yards when they heard the powerful impact of the crash.

"God lee, y'all heard that?" One of the guys said.

A woman replied in a startled tone, "Oh my lord that there sounded wrong, we need to go and see what happened."

"Yo ass just wants to be nosey," the man replied, causing the group to laugh. Angrily the woman responded, "Shut yo ole raggedy ass up. Ain't nobody trying to be no damn nosey. I know you heard how bad that crash sounded," as she stood up from the hood of a car and began to walk in the direction of the sound of the collision.

"Mary! Aye! Stop playing girl and bring yo black ass back over here man, that ain't got nothing to do with you."

"Shut yo ass up Greg," she yelled while making her way down the street.

Drinking her beer, she looked north up the Avenue but didn't see anything. Turning her head south to find the crash she nearly choked on her beer as she frantically screamed out, "Greg! Greg! Call the ambulance! Call the ambulance! This car is flipped over. Hurry up."

"What!?" The man Greg yelled out because he couldn't hear her from such a far distance. Another guy replied, "Aye, man, I think she said to call the ambulance."

"Call the ambulance? Man, what the hell this crazy ass woman is talking about?" the guy named Greg said as he stood up from the black milk crate he was sitting on. "Come on y'all, let's go see what she talking about." As they made their way down to the corner of the block, they could see the woman Mary shaking her right hand vigorously and pacing in distress.

Once they made it to the corner, all their faces turned gray as they looked at a car flipped over on its hood and a semi-truck wedged on a median barely missing a disastrous collision with a concrete beam holding up the Metrorail track.

Slowly and clumsily the driver of the semi slowly got down from the truck, but in total shock, he could only cover his mouth with one hand and rub his head with the other as he fell to his knees.

"I told you it was bad," the woman said while crying. "Go back and call the ambulance Mary. Everybody else, let's go!" Greg commanded as he and the two other men raced down the avenue to see if everybody involved in the car accident was okay.

Approaching the scene, they ran up to the truck driver who was laying in the street, 'unconscious' from the shock of the crash. "Yo, you okay?" Greg said to the truck driver but he was out cold, so he didn't respond. "Y'all two pick him up and put him in the grass over there on the median. I'ma go see if anybody in the other car is hurt," Greg ordered the men. Greg then rushed over to the car and bent down to see how many people were in the car, but to his surprise, there was only one person.

Pop's body was slumped over in the back seat so Greg couldn't see his face. Greg reached his hand in and slightly turned Pop's head so that Pop's wouldn't suffocate on the seat cushion. But once Greg turned Pop's head, his eyes grew as wide as the moon in sheer horror.

The other men moved in on the car and tried to see if they could help, but as they too looked upon the wreckage, their faces turned sour with grief. One of the guys stepped back and yelled out to the woman and few other people that had come out to see what was going on, "Aye, this Diana boy over here. Somebody go call her right now, Hurry up!"

"Alright, let's see if we can get him out," Greg said to the other men, but being that the car was so badly mangled, they couldn't find an angle to pull pops out of the wreckage. Almost twenty minutes had gone by, and the ambulance still hadn't shown up. By now the homeless guy who pops had given the change to had already shared key details with the group of onlookers about how the crash happened.

Standing at a distance from the accident site they had all assumed that the driver of the car was already deceased, while they watched over the truck driver to make sure he didn't try to leave. That's when the woman Mary started to cry out in dismay, "Greg! Greg! I think he's still alive I just heard him scream for help. Oh, my gosh Greg. Y'all got to go back over there and get him."

"Mary, Mary, come here baby calm down, calm down, it's okay. He's gone baby, I'm sorry - I'm sorry, it's going to be alright, just trust me. The ambulance on the way - they going to get him," he said to her as he reached in to hug his hysterically crying girlfriend who was obviously traumatized by the entire situation.

"No, Greg. I heard him - I heard him," she said while crying on his shoulder. That's when all of a sudden, a faint and excruciating moan for "help" echoed from Pops who was presumed dead. Everyone quickly stopped what they were doing and looked at each other. That's when an even louder shout for help was heard. Without hesitation, the men dashed back over to the car in hopes that they would be able to help pops.

"Hey there now, you awake there boy? We're here. It's me Mr. Greg from fifteenth talking to you. We called the ambulance, and they say they on their way, so just stick in here with us baby boy," he said to pops in a calming voice. He was hoping that by talking to pops, he would help him remain conscious long enough until the ambulance arrived. But it's the hood, so there wasn't any telling on how much longer it was going to take before they got there.

"Alright now baby boy look-a-here, we need you to hang in there until the ambulance gets here okay? We ain't going nowhere until they come and get you up out of this mess, Alright? You hear me," Greg said.

With no response, he screamed out, "Aye! You wake up, hear? Don't you be going to sleep on me! You strong and you gon' have to keep fighting until you make it up out of this, you just need to keep your head to the side and try not to move too much."

Still, with another stint of silence, Greg reached in and gently poured a bottle of cold water over pops face. "Aye, c'mon on now - I need you to say something, speak to me man, let me know you're alright." But in so much agonizing pain all pops could do was give out a somber moan.

Crouched he asked, "Hey soldier, can you feel your fingers?" Pops replied with a gentle, "Yeah."

"That's good - that's good," Greg said, "but how about your legs, can you feel your legs?" Again, with another soft reply, Pops sighed the word, "No." Greg then stood up slowly, walked away from the car and began pacing with his hands has behind his head.

One of the guys asked, "Greg what's wrong man? What he'd say to you?" Slowly turning around to face the other gentlemen standing with him, he shook his head and uttered, "I think he's paralyzed."

"What you mean?" they all said to Greg.

"He can't feel his legs man. He can't feel his freaking legs," Greg replied, before kicking a broken head light on the ground and at that very moment the sound of the ambulance came driving in.

Police quickly hopped out of their cars and attempted to secure a parameter around the scene. You could hear the commotion from the small crowd of people cursing and expressing their frustrations about how long it took for them to arrive as they moved back behind the yellow crime scene tape.

Pulling up to the site of the crash almost an hour

later, all my grandmother Diana could see was flashing police lights, yellow tape that roped off nearly two city blocks, my dad's vehicle in shambles and a white sheet covering what appeared to be a body. Instantly her heart began to melt as her eyes flooded with tears, leaving her stomach with that critical hollowness of grief.

My older cousin Aaliyah parked the car just about three hundred feet away from the group of people standing behind the crime scene tape so that she and my grandmother could walk over. Woodenly walking towards the accident scene, my grandmother grew an unbearable feeling of sickness that filled her throat.

As she moved in closer, she could see folk crying and trying to hold each other together. Pointing in her direction Mr. Greg directed a detective towards her.

The detective approached her and said, "Excuse me, Ma'am, how are you? My name is Detective Catheryn Mejia-Perez, I am the lead investigator here at tonight's scene. I was informed that you might be related to one of the individuals involved in this evening's unfortunate event. Would you be kind enough to assist me in identifying the deceased victim of this evening's accident?"

With a deep gulp of emptiness, tears dripped from her eyes as she cleared her throat and reluctantly replied, "Yes ma'am, I will."

CHAPTER 2

Mangos and Sunshine

"LET ME SEE you pump them thangs, shake that Uhm... do do brown," was the electrifying verse to an Uncle Luke track that seemed to almost hypnotize people at every party or summer cookout. As soon as that song came on you knew it was about to go down, and when I say go down - I mean it was about to be a whole lot of rump shaking going on. Every woman old and young would immediately stop whatever it was that they were doing. It didn't matter if it was somebody aunty fixing the hungry, energetic kids a plate of hot dogs, pork n beans, with lays potato chips or a little girl jumping around in a bounce house. They all ran in a dash to form a circle where all of them would dance when this song came on. They would start by first flipping their shoes off to the side, then pull up their shorts or dresses so they could spread their legs while gradually kicking their feet outwards to prop themselves into position - and before you knew it - the whole party had made a circle around them as they danced their hearts away.

Growing up as a kid in 'Da City,' well that's what we call Liberty City down here in Miami. Every day was filled with excitement, and it seemed like the sun would never stop shining. The woody aroma of burning barbecue grills saturated the vibrant Liberty City air, as the dry, scorching heat of the sun made everyone thirsty and happy when the evening breeze gracefully swung through right before dawn.

Where kids would be begging their parents for money, as soon as, they heard the ice cream truck coming or chasing after it just to ride on the back of the truck when the driver wasn't looking.

These were the times when the days got so hot that my grandma would tell my cousins and I, "If y'all come back in this house one more damn time, y'all gon' stay in." So instead of going back inside of the house when we needed to use the bathroom. We would go around back, find a spot to pee in a bush and afterward run to the side of the house to quickly wash our hands or grab a drink of the warm water from the outside water hose, and then got right back to playing.

Like many other kids that were growing up in Da City, we all lived at home with almost all of our immediate family members. Being so young in the 90's, it never actually dawned on me that the only reason most of lived this way was because we were poor.

Yeah, occasionally you'd have that one kid whose feet would stink so badly because he's been wearing the same shoes since the third grade, so we'd pick on him or that one group of sisters who used to share clothes and would lie about it – so we'd call them dirty.

But since we all lived in the same neighborhood, attended the same schools, in the end, we had no choice but to be friends and have each other's backs. Because let someone outside of our hood decide to have a problem with any one of us, they'd find out quick that they'd messed with the wrong people and we'd all be there to put up a fight.

At home, my Grandma Sheryl was the head of the house. A single mom living in a Two-bedroom, one-bathroom apartment on the second floor of a rundown apartment building in the heart of Liberty City.

She had two daughters, a son, two grandsons and her older brother - my great uncle Sherman all packed in one unit. Although my uncle Sherman was her older brother, she had to take care of him because of his mental disability ever since her mother passed away. So, when uncle Sherman got his disability check, she would use most his money to pay the bills and then give him a hundred dollars to spend on himself each month. I guess giving him a hundred dollars helped clear her conscious of taking advantage of him.

Grandma Sheryl was a short-tempered woman who worked overnight shifts as a nurse's assistant down at Jackson Hospital. When she would come back home in the morning, she would head right to her room, lock the door and go straight to sleep. During the day living in her house, everybody was expected to either be at school or find somewhere outside to go all day.

Especially on the weekends when she cleaned and cooked Sunday dinner. She didn't want to hear a peep from anybody in that house, not even the sound of the refrigerator turning on. And you better not had stepped on that floor after she just mopped it, you were destined to get something thrown at you.

Even though my Grandma was strict, she made sure that she took care of everything in the house and everybody in the family. Which is probably why I always felt happy being able to come home and show everyone what I had done in school each day.

In elementary, I was seriously involved in art class. So, whenever I had the opportunity to do an art project I would always do it in honor of my family but most of the times I dedicated my crafts to my mommy because she was my best friend, my everything at that age.

Moms were all that I had ever known in this world. I knew that my father passed away when I was a baby, but she didn't talk about him that much. She was the most beautiful woman that I had ever seen. Short, boney, skin the complexion of ground cinnamon and as smooth as the cocoa butter lotion she used every day.

Her eyes were perfectly round and full of sunshine each time she gazed upon me. Her signature hairstyle was a red dyed short cut at the time, so people in the neighborhood decided to nickname her "Red."

Moms and I were super close. Not having enough room in the house, my mother and I had to sleep in one of two twin beds in a small room she shared with my aunty. While my uncle Sherman slept on the sofa and my uncle Maurice had to make a pallet on the living room floor whenever he decided to come home.

Before we went to sleep each night, my mom would always spray on this soothing vanilla scented body spray that made me feel at ease. I would hop in the bed after I finished playing with my toys in the tub, scoot down in the bed with my mom's feet towards my head, clench tightly onto her curled up legs and positioned myself to fall asleep, just thinking of how thankful I was to have her as my "Queen."

Being outside in the neighborhood all day is pretty much how my younger cousin Jaleel and I were able to get closer. Only a few months older than he was, at times we felt more like brothers being that we had lived with each other our entire lives. Jaleel was my main man, even though we'd fight over the smallest things like who's taking a bath first or him wanting to watch football when I wanted to watch cartoons. We stuck together like gum on the bottom of a shoe and always had each other's back no matter what.

It was a typical hot and extremely humid day in the neighborhood as everybody enjoyed being outside in the Miami weather. On my block, there was an intense neighborhood rivalry football game going on in the middle of the street that everybody came out to watch. It was my block against some dudes from the projects that had been talking smack for the longest about how their squad would beat our block in football.

Wrapping up in the bathroom scrubbing down the tub as fast as I could because the game was about to start downstairs. It was supposed to be Jaleel's' day to clean, but since he was about to play in the match today, he asked me to do it for him. Once I finished, I hurried down the stairs of the apartment, headed to the candy lady that lived beneath us to buy a fifty-cent Lily Dilly or "frozen cup" as we call it in Da City and a bag of Cheddar Cheese Ruffles.

Seeing my lil cousin out there getting ready to ball, I got excited because the older guys didn't allow us jits to play until we got in middle school. But my lil cousin was small and quick, so they figured it'd be smart of them to use him on the team since he'd probably be hard to catch. Even though I was good at football, I always chose not to play whenever I got asked because sports weren't my thing.

As I walked towards the sideline, which was a small crack in the ground that separated the street from the sidewalk, this kid from the other neighborhood walked up on me and smacked my orange flavored frozen cup right out of my hand, then took off running.

Dropping my bag of chips in absolute fury, I chased after him as we ran onto the next block until I finally got close enough to grab his shirt. We were about the same size, but I was pissed off as we grappled with each other I put him in the headlock.

He laid there giggling saying, "Alright, Alright, you got me, man, you got me. I was just playing." Slightly releasing my grip, I told him, "That – wasn't – funny – you dummy," before pushing him away and getting up to dust the dirt off my legs.

Still laughing he said, "Man, you soft. I could've beat you if I wanted to." As we both stood in front of this abandoned house, a whispery voice called from the far-right of me.

"Aye! What y'all doing man? Come on before that old lady sees y'all." For a second, I stood there confused because I wasn't sure if I was about to get jumped by some dudes that I didn't know but then as I looked closer, I saw that the kid whispering had a shirt pouched with a ton of ripe mangos.

"Come on," the dumb kid who I'd put in the headlock said, "We getting mangos from the backyard." Unenthusiastically, I hesitated because I didn't want to get jumped nor did I want to get in trouble for being over here without asking my mama but I figured shoot if I take her back some of these mangos she won't be mad. So skeptically, I went ahead and followed behind him towards the back of the abandoned house.

Tip toeing through the overgrown grass, I could hear others whispering to each other and moving around in the backyard. Once I got back there one of the guys came up and said, "What is he doing back here? Who he is?" That's when Dummy said, he straight this my dawg. He lives on the other block where yo brother them playing football."

"Oh okay," he said before coming towards me to dap me up then asking, "Aye, you know how to climb trees?"

Feeling relieved that I wasn't about to get jumped, I said, "Yeah - I climb trees all the time." It was like I made his day with that response because he silently clapped his hands and said "Good, now we got more people to get mangos off the tree," while slowly rubbing his hands together.

"You scared?" Dummy asked me before taking me over to where two other guys were counting the stash and sorting out the good mangos for themselves. "Naw I ain't scared," I told him. But in fact, I was a bit worried about my mama coming outside to look for me, and I wasn't there. If that happened, I could almost guarantee I had a whooping waiting on me.

My goal was to get these mangos and get out of here

as quickly as possible. Reaching in to pick up a mango from the stash the two guys were sorting, one of them sitting on the concrete porch sorting said, "Nun Uh Yo! You better get your own mangos - these ours. Don't nobody know you like that jit."

Slightly intimidated, I backed off because I didn't want to do anything that might've caused me to get jumped by these guys. That's when Dummy said, "Yeah man you got to get your own, but I'll go with you though cause I ain't get none yet either."

"How we suppose to get em?" I said. He laughed and then sarcastically replied, "We got to climb the tree, how else?" Looking around in the back yard, I realized that there wasn't a tree back here, it was just the huge branches from the tree next door that extended over into this backyard.

Nervously I whispered, "How we supposed to get in the tree? We got to jump the gate?" I wasn't about to go in that lady yard because she might've had a dog or if we got caught she might call the police on us, and we'd get in trouble. The guy counting said, "No fool. Y'all got to get on the roof and then get in the tree."

Afraid to ask another dumb question, I looked up and wondered, "Now how in the hell are we going to get on this roof?" and before you knew it the kid that dapped me up hopped on these metal protection bars extending in front of a window, pulled himself up so that he could stand on top of them. He then leaped across onto a small ledge that covered the back porch before squirming himself onto the rooftop and climbed into the tree using one of the thick branches extended over.

My nerves began to jitter because I wasn't too sure about this now that I'd seen what he had to do to get up there. Glancing at the kid move slowly through the tree like Tarzan, Dummy hit my shoulder and uttered, "You scared ain't you?" I'm sure my face showed it as I weakly replied, "Huh?"

"Yeah man, you scared," he said in a disappointed tone. "How about you just stand down here and catch the mangos when they fall off the tree, alright?"

"Naw I ain't scared. I'll go up there," I replied to redeem myself, knowing how much I didn't want to get up there. But Dummy insisted, "Naw you just stay down here while I go up and knock them down. This way we'll be able to get more."

Graciously thankful, I said to him, "Alright that sounds like a smart plan, I got you." He turned around and walked over to the starting point of getting onto the roof to slowly make his way up. One of the other kids that had this nappy high-top fade stopped sorting because he wanted to get more mangos too, came over to help me.

We waited as they crept through the tree like iguanas and like rain drops falling from the sky, the mangos came pouring down one by one. Racing to find the camouflaged mangos in the high grass, we had to take our shirts off, creating makeshift pouches to carry the massive bundles of mangos.

"Aye! Y'all hurry up before the lady come," the kid with the high-top screeched up to the other guys still up in the tree.

"Stop acting like a lil girl," the kid who initially asked why was I there said, before he announced to us, "Aye, y'all see that whole bunch of mangos right there pointing at a cluster of delicious looking ripe mangoes. I'ma shake the whole branch as hard as I can, then y'all grab the ones that fall so we can leave but that big one right there - that one mine."

Standing in the tree, he extended his left leg out towards the branch beneath him and started to kick down on it, to force the patch of mangos to fall.

"Aye! They not falling," the high-top kid on the ground with me yelled up. "Hold on," the kid in the tree replied, as he carefully shifted himself onto a much lower branch where he could stand firmly with the both of his feet. Gripping a sturdy branch above him, he gently began to bounce on the branch as if it was a diving board at Charles Hadley Park.

The leaves of the tree rattled as he asked us, "Any of them fall off yet?" We responded, "Naw - not yet but they look like they about to fall though." Seeing how close he was to make them fall, he gradually started to shake the limb a lot harder, and finally one dropped.

"Aye, keep shaking," I said, "One just fell." Bending the branch so far, it seemed like he was up there jumping on a trampoline. Within seconds, more began to drop down to the ground, so we raced to pick them up. Not realizing that he was starting to apply way too much pressure on the tree branch. SNAP! The huge tree branch broke off, sending him and the mangos hurling towards the ground.

"Oh shit," we said while dashing out of the way trying to avoid getting crushed by the branch as it made its way down. Concerned and slightly shaken, we rushed over to see if he was alright but immediately he got up from the hard fall laughing and said, "Y'all boys seen that? Man, I thought I was finna die y'all boys."

The rest of us began to laugh as we became relieved that he didn't get seriously hurt. We hurried to pick up the remaining mangos that had fallen because as the tree snapped we heard the lady next door yell through a small window,

"WHO THE HELL IS IN MY BACKYARD? I'm calling the police on y'all lil badasses."

Hauling tail, we slid through a small tear in the fence as we headed down the sidewalk running bare-chested with a bunch of mangos in the pouches of our shirts. Our socks and shoes were covered in those little green prickly things we called sticky birds.

"Aye man, what's yo name?" the kid I called

Dummy, said to me. But before I could even reply he said, "Man, I'ma just call you Cornbread."

"Cornbread?" I restated in confusion. "What you going to call me cornbread for?"

In a teasing voice he said, "Because, you sweet, that's why," as he playfully attempted to trip me. "Man, you play too much," I said in an aggressive tone trying to gain my respect, "And you got me messed up. Ain't nobody sweet jit, you sweet." Although he was kind of annoying, I did think Dummy was an alright dude. Shoot, I nearly forgot that he made me drop my freaking frozen cup since we had all these delicious mangos to munch on but the memory was still too fresh.

"So, what school you go to?" he asked me, as we walked through a shortcut behind my apartment building that led us back onto my block. Again, I didn't get the opportunity to answer another one of his questions because the kid that fell out of the tree yelled out, "Aye! Y'all hear that? It sounds like somebody arguing over there," referring to the people who were on my block.

High-top replied, "Yo, that sound like yo brother," sparking tree falling kid to start jogging through the narrow patch of space that ran along the side of my apartment building.

When we go out of the cut, we could see that indeed it was his brother arguing with one of the other guys from the football game that lived on my block. The argument was started because the kids' brother had stepped out of bounds about twenty feet back, so their fourth and long touchdown didn't count for the win.

Games like these got intense, so it was normal for a scuffle or two to break out during the games, but guys would normally get right back to playing ball. But by the looks of things, this game wasn't about to continue at all. One of the guys that were playing on the team representing my block got frustrated that the other guys didn't want to take the option of turnover on downs, which means the other guys would have to give the ball up or to just redo the play from the original spot of the ball. So, he threw the football on top of the roof of another apartment building.

Within seconds, this started a full-on brawl, between the two teams. Standing on the south side of the street, I could see my little cousin sitting on top of a green Mitsubishi, to move out of the way of the much older and larger guys before he got swung on or knocked out.

I yelled out to him, "Jaleel – come across the street." Looking at me, I could see in his eyes that it didn't faze him - not one bit. "Jaleel, hurry up man!" I said to him as he slowly crept down from the roof of the car.

Nervous that the other kids would now try to fight us too, my heart began pounding as I felt that electrifying pulse of adrenaline rush from my stomach to my throat. I looked around at them bracing myself for something to pop off, but they looked just as worried as I did.

"Dang man, he always doing this, we can never go nowhere without him trying to fight somebody man," the tree falling kid said angrily. The kid with the high top replied, "Man we told you this was going to happen. We said, 'Watch when we get over there yo brother try to start something.' He always does this crap man crap. Shoot I ain't jumping in this time."

Doubtful of them, I stepped back again and screamed at my cousin once more, "Jaleel! Get yo behind over here before yo mama beat yo ass man, dang." It was like he was moving in slow motion, while everything else surrounding us was on fast forward.

Still fighting, the kid's brother got punched in the jaw and fell hard to the floor causing everyone to shout "Oou." Embarrassed that this just happened to him, he got up and ran towards a wrapped-up shirt that was lying next to a light pole, where he then pulled out a gun.

It was like watching something straight out of a movie because as soon as he turned around pointing the gun, everybody standing around and fighting in the street, took off running for their life.

POP! POP! POP! POP! POP! POP! POP!

Frighten by the explosive sound of the gunfire, the four of us hauled tail back through the small passage on the side of the building, pushing and bumping into each other as we frantically sought a safe place to hide. "Go! Go! Move! Move!" we screamed to one another until we finally ducked down and hid underneath the staircase behind the apartment.

Breathing hard, we all looked at one another in complete shock as we waited for things to clear. "You alright?" Dummy asked me while wiping the nervous sweat from his eyes. "Yeah - I'm good," I replied to him. "You think yo brother them gone?" he asked the other kid. "Yeah, I think they gone. They ain't shooting no more so they must be gone," the other kid whispered. "Alright, I'ma peep out to see if we can leave," Dummy responded.

Crouching, he cautiously peeped out to make sure that the coast was clear before he waved his hand at the rest of us, signaling that everything looked straight and we were alright to come out of hiding. Slowly moving from behind the fetid staircase, we walked along the side the gate attempting to retrieve some of the mangos that had fallen as we ran. That's when dummy put his right hand out and intensely whispered, "Aye, y'all boys stop. I think somebody got shot."

Our hearts instantly filled with fear as one of the guys whispered, "Who is it?" as his legs visibly started to tremble. "I don't know," he replied, "It's some kid wearing an orange shirt. He in the street bleeding and he ain't moving."

Hearing those words from his mouth caused my heart to jump from chest directly to my gut as I gasped, "Orange shirt!?"

"Yeah, he got on an orange shirt. I think he dead cause he ain't moving," he said in a saddened tone.

Frantically I yelled out, "MOVE!" as I forcefully shoved my way through their thin bodies, making my way towards the sidewalk. I abruptly stopped in complete disbelief of what my eyes were seeing. My throat was beginning to close in, my stomach dropped, my ears rang with a sound like the one you'd hear in a room filled with silence, and the world I once knew seemed to come to a standstill.

Here I was, trapped in an unwanted moment of time that I would have never predicted. The sunshine stretching down had never seemed duller as I slowly walked towards the body of Jaleel lying drenched in his blood on the concrete road. My mind was numbed as I kneeled to grab hold of his head. Staring into his innocent face and blank stare, I could still see that same worry free attitude he wore.

I called out to him as my eyes welled into a puddle of tears, "Cousin, come on man wake up. I told you to come across the street," I cried out. My nose was running with snot, as I shook his body in hopes that he'd respond to me.

"Jaleel, come on man wake up. We're going to call the ambulance, and everything is going to be alright. Please, just wake up," I pleaded, but still, he laid there with no sound of life as his body flopped around sluggishly in my arms.

Struggling and filled with an urgency I attempted to pick him up into my arms so that I could get him back across the street. But before I could do so, an older guy from the neighborhood ran up to me, slowly pulled Jaleel from my arms, moving me away from his body and then carried me away.

The distraught cries of my aunty "echoed" through the neighborhood as I laid hopelessly in the back seat of a parked Cadillac. I cried so much that my eyes burned and my soul felt as empty as ever. The only thing I could think of as I watched them carry my cousin's body away was, "Why?

"Why did this have to happen to me and why did it have to happen to my cousin? He's my best friend, my little brother. Why couldn't this have been somebody else? It was my fault because if I had never stayed over there to get those mangos, I would've been able to protect him and none of this would've ever happened."

CHAPTER 3

Misery Loves Company

THE DAYS SWIFTLY faded away as my lil cousin's death began to settle in. It seems that every other family was scarred by a violent death and mine was not an exception. Growing up in the Da City, it was both common, yet unexpected. The reality of it happening began to take a toll on the family. Sometimes I'd be excited about doing something and get ready to tell Jaleel all about it, but then I realize that he wasn't here anymore. At times, I thought I would see him in the shadows when I woke up in the middle of the night, so I'd end up staying awake until the morning. On the other hand, my aunty – man she was going through it. I watched her as she cried herself to sleep on some nights, just talking about how she missed her baby and why they had to take him away from her. It was so bad that for a long time it was hard for her to eat, sleep or even breathe at times because Jaleel was pretty much all she had in life.

So, for her to lose him, it was as if the world had ripped her spirit right out of her body because she couldn't figure out how she was going to live without him. Not being able to deal with living at grandma house she decided that it was time for her to move out into her own place. Aunty felt like the memories that lived in the apartment were overwhelming, and was the reason she was becoming miserable, so she left.

I had known she wanted to leave, but when I got out of school one day and saw that all her stuff was gone. My soul began to ache because Aunty was my favorite and she always made me feel good. At times, I felt like she was the only one that understood me when no one else did.

"Who was going to massage my head and cook mac-n-cheese for me now?" It was like my world was slowly falling apart, becoming more and more vacant each day. Growing up without my Pops, then Jaleel was gone, now Aunty went away too; my world was gradually being taken away bit by bit.

My mom and I were still living with my grandma for a while, but when things started to get rough around the house, and when she couldn't get a job, my grandma ended up giving us the boot and kicking us out.

Grandma Sheryl was all about her rules and since my mom couldn't follow them and Aunty wasn't there to cover for her anymore, Grandma said we had to go. Moms tried to put up a good front to get Grandma to let us stay, but after one too many warnings about having too many folks running in and out of the house, plus the fact that moms seemed to always have a problem with helping pay the bills, Grandma was fed up.

Although I was so young, I could still feel the eerie tension that settled throughout the house showing me that things were only getting worse with the family as we all seemed to become increasingly disconnected from one another.

When we initially got kicked out, we ended up moving in with one of my mama's friends. When that didn't work out too well, we then began bouncing from motel to motel. It wasn't all that bad to me because I felt like we were going on road trips all the time. But, at the same time, we could never find somewhere to stay for good and always had to be on the move.

Every time we would relocate moms would always to say to me, "This our last time moving," because she had found a new job and she was looking at some new places for us to move in. My favorite thing was when she'd hype me up about how she'll be able to take me shopping, so that I could get all the new toys I wanted and how she was going to get me a bike this way I could ride around the new neighborhood with all the other kids.

She had me sold I tell you, but, for one reason or another, none of those things ever seemed to happen. We'd still end up moving to another motel, and she'd end up selling me the same story that I would always buy into all over again.

I mean I loved my mommy, so I always listened to her, and of course, I believed that everything she was saying to me had to be genuine and would eventually happen sooner than later. It had to get better, right? I could not imagine life getting any worse.

The days were bleak, but I was beginning to feel like I was maturing faster because, at the motels, my mama would leave me there by myself forcing me to be a little more responsible.

I remember one Saturday afternoon; I was sitting down on the edge of the bed watching some show on TV about lions chasing prey in the African Safari when she busted open the door all excited, smiling widely when she said to me.

"Son get up! I got good news."

Surprised and anxious to know why she was moving so quickly, I said to her. "What happened ma?"

"I was talking to yo Aunty, and she said she wanted us to come live with her, so we going to go live with Aunty Shay, she told me."

Surprised because I hadn't seen Aunty Shay in a

long time, I said to her, "For real ma, like for real for real?"

"Boy, didn't I just say we were - now hurry up and go get in the shower so we can pack up. By the time, I get out the tub after you I will call a cab so that we can go."

Man, I tell you. I jumped off that bed so fast and ran into the bathroom to strip naked out of my clothes; you would've thought I was in a track meet. I was so excited that I turned on the shower and hopped right in the tub forgetting that the water in motel took some time to warm up. So, when I jumped in the shower, that cold water splashed my chest, and I nearly busted my behind trying to bounce back out of that tub.

Sitting on the toilet waiting, I began to sing to myself, "We going to Aunty house, we going to Aunty house." After a minute or so, I reached my hand back behind the shower curtain to see if the water had warmed up a little. It wasn't scorching hot like I usually like it, but I didn't care, I just wanted to hurry up so we could go to Aunty Shay house.

Moms got out of the tub, and as she said, she called the Society Cab. I heard a honk come from outside, peeping out the dusty blinds of the window curtain I saw this black and green taxi outside. I screamed towards the bathroom where my mom was trying to gel down her hair edges.

"Mama, the Society Cab outside."

She yelled back, "Alright, go grab your stuff and ask

him to come help us when you get out there." With cab drivers help, I threw our things in the backseat of the cab as the driver helped put some stuff in the trunk.

It was close to three o'clock when we finally pulled up in front of my aunty house, and it felt like we had just landed on Paradise Island. When the car stopped, my mom told me to knock on the door as she paid the fee for the cab ride.

Knocking on the door, I could smell the scent of vanilla oozing through the cracks of the doorway. The door opened, and the ice-cold breeze of the a/c slapped me right in the face. "Hey Nephew, I miss you baby, where yo mama?" Aunty said to me, as I reached in for a hug. "She outside, she's paying the cabman I said." That's when I heard moms calling my name to return so I could help bring the bags into the house.

Aunty lived in a small duplex, but it looked nice, smelled good and was always clean. I ain't never have my own room but finding out that I would be able to sleep in the living room by myself still made me feel excited that I could have my own little space.

I tell you things just couldn't get any better. But, in a matter of weeks, it would all be short lived cause one day my old girl left me alone at Aunty Shay's place by myself, while she went out to handle whatever business she had to handle.

By now I was used to the routine, so it didn't bother

me none when my mom would come tell me, "Alright, I'm about to leave so you already know what to do. Keep that door closed, don't let anybody in here and if somebody come knocking don't answer it. You already know where the food is, so make sure you eat something while I'm gone."

Then she would gently kiss me on the forehead, tell me, "I ain't going to be out for long, I'ma be right back. I'm going around the corner for a lil bit," as she'd playfully smack me on the butt, rise from kneeling down and head towards the door to hit the road.

When she left, I can't even lie I was always a little bit scared because I hated being by myself but at the same time, I was somewhat excited as well. It allowed me to have some peace and quiet time to myself, but sometimes the noises around the house would creep me out because I felt like something was out to get me.

Once, shortly after Jaleel passed, I was dreaming that we were playing and out of nowhere I woke but when I tried to move, I couldn't. I laid face down on the couch feeling as though like something was holding me down and preventing me from screaming out for help.

Fearfully, I closed my eyes begging for whatever that was happening to me at that moment to just stop. I tell you no lie, I don't know if I was tripping off a nightmare or not, but as soon as I finished saying that to myself, in my peripheral view, I could see a shadow of something move quickly towards the kitchen as I rose frightened and gasping for air.

I told my mama about it, but she just brushed it off saying that it was a nightmare, but I remember my grandma saying that when you experience something like that, it meant that the devil was riding on your back. From that point on, I always slept with my back to the wall so that I could see in the kitchen.

But on the day that moms left me alone at aunty house, every few minutes I would peep out of the window to see if she'd be standing outside talking or walking down. After a few hours had passed and there was still no sign of her, I eventually gave up on waiting for her.

With my stomach starting to growl, I walked over to the kitchen fix get myself a bowl of cereal. Too short to reach on top of the fridge, I grabbed a chair from the dining table, pushed it against the fridge and pulled the cereal down. I fixed my first bowl but took the box with me and sat on the couch with my blanket watching cartoons until I fell asleep.

Knocked out cold on the sofa, I felt a slight nudge on my shoulder. Initially, I thought it was one of the couch pillows falling onto the floor, so I moved slightly and dusted myself off. That's when I got nudged a little harder and heard a soft whisper telling me to, "Wake up." Slowly opening my crusted eyes, I thought to myself, "It was about time my mom had come back," but when I got a good look, I realized that it was my aunty. She had just gotten off work around seven o'clock, and the look on her face was one of those eyebrows raised, confused mad faces.

You know the look on someone's face when they're trying to figure out what the heck is going on, so they give a situation the benefit of the doubt before they start acting a fool? That's what her face showed.

I could see the flames burning inside of her eyes as she said to me, "Nephew, wake up!"

Sitting upright on the couch, I rubbed my dry eyes, as I stated in a groggy voice, "Hey, Aunty."

"Where is yo mama?" She asked me, trying to restrain her imminent anger. "Uh, she told me she was going around the corner, she'll be right back Aunty."

"Around the corner?" She muttered irritably. "How long she been out?"

"Since like eleven o'clock," I said to her while yawning and stretching my arms. Confused she replied, "Eleven o'clock? What in the hell? Nun Uh, I don't know what kind of party she thinks this is but not today, not in my damn house. Get up nephew," she said to me even more irritated than before

"Did you even take a bath yet?" She asked me. "No Aunty," I replied. "Have you even had anything to eat since she been gone?" Aunty uttered.

"Yes, I had some cereal Aunty," I replied. She closed her eyes and started shaking her head before demanding me to fix the couch and go wash out my bowl so that I could then take a shower.

After giving her instructions, you could hear her hard footsteps collide with the floor as she angrily stormed off to her bedroom. From the living room, I could hear her mumbling curse words and express her frustration about what I had just told her. I sadly thought to myself, "Please don't make us have to move again Aunty."

Concerned because I wasn't sure about what was going to happen next, I went into the kitchen to wash the bowl out and made my way to the bathroom for my bath. While in the shower, I could smell the scent of fresh grease cooking on the stove and could tell that Aunty was about to whip up some of her good ole fried chicken.

I hurried to the bathroom because I wanted to make sure I got my plate while it was still hot. Ain't nothing better than when your food so hot, that you have to move your mouth around like a fish gulping water to not burn your tongue. Fresh out the shower, I threw on my favorite ninja turtle pajamas and walked to the kitchen to see if Aunty was good.

"Dang Aunty Shay, that chicken smell good," I said to start a conversation, but Aunty just stood there flipping chicken in the floor and dropping it in the hot grease. Since she ignored me, I figured shoot, let me give her a hug so she knows I love her and hopefully it would help her stop being mad. But as soon as she saw me move from by the opening of the kitchen towards her she stopped me.

"Get out of my kitchen. I will let you know when the food is ready. Go sit down in the living room and watch TV" she said to me, without even turning around.

Now I knew she wasn't in a good mood because people only say your full name when they either pissed off or frustrated about something. But me being me I still attempted to make her happy, so I replied, "Ok Aunty, I love you," but she just kept on cooking and didn't pay any mind to my attempts to ease her angry mood.

Disappointed because I could tell that she was still bothered, I turned around and went to the couch so I could leave her alone while I watched some cartoons. Almost fifteen minutes later I heard her yell, "Come grab some of this newspaper from under the sink and put it on the floor in front of the TV." Being a kid, I wasn't allowed to eat my food at her neat dining the table; I had to eat on the floor because she didn't want me to mess up her table mats.

Hearing those perfect words come from her mouth, I knew it was time to get my grub on and man I was happy. I was starving and couldn't wait to get my hands on some of Aunty good ole golden brown crispy, crunchy chicken. I promise she made some of the best fried chicken I've ever tasted.

Rubbing my hands together, I bounced up from sitting cross-legged on the floor and grabbed some newspaper from under the sink. I always grabbed the comic section so that I could read them as I ate - put that thang on the floor in front of the TV and anxiously awaited as I sat back down with my legs crossed until she called me to get my plate.

"Come on!" That was her next signal." Grabbing my plate, I saw that she had whipped up some fried chicken, rice, and baked beans. "Thank you, Aunty," I said her. Go put your plate down and get the Kool-Aid out the refrigerator so I can pour you something to drink" she told me.

After we both sat there and ate Aunty cleaned up the kitchen, she went to her room to get her night clothes so she could take a shower and when she finished walked right into her bedroom closing the door behind her. I caught the "Itis," as the cold air was making me sleepy again. Everything seemed to be just fine even though it was now close to ten o'clock with still no sign of my mama.

Near midnight, Aunty came out of her room to turn off the TV in the living room where I slept. I heard her open the door to the room where my mama slept and made a deep sigh. She came back over and reminded me, "Nephew, get up and go pee before you go to bed."

Not feeling like moving out of my comfortable spot, I reluctantly replied, "Okay Aunty," before getting up. When I got back from the bathroom, I laid down, pulled the covers over my head because it was dark and I wasn't trying to see anything scary. I laid there lonely and could only think about was where my mama was? I hope nothing bad happened to her.

It wasn't the first time she had left me alone, but it was the first time she had left me and not returned the same day. I began to quietly pout, and sort of cry as all the worst ideas that could happen to her popped into my head and the thoughts of losing her just like Jaleel terrified me I sat there praying and asking God to bring her back home safely.

When the next morning came, Aunty walked into the other bedroom again to see if mama had come back and to her displeasure moms wasn't there. Pretending to be asleep, I smelled the irresistible aroma pancakes and sausages being made, so I got up from the couch to use the bathroom and then walked into the kitchen doorway.

"Good Morning Aunty Shay," I said as I leaned on the wall by the kitchen opening. "Good Morning," she nonchalantly replied to me. I figured that she was still in a bad mood since my mama didn't make it back home last night.

Feeling her frustration, I slowly turned around and went to the bathroom to brush my teeth. Her sink was kind of high, so I had to stand on the toilet to lean over the sink to reach the knobs for the water. Rinsing the toothpaste from my mouth, I splashed my face with water when I heard a loud banging sound coming from the front door.

Boom! Boom! Boom! Boom! "It's mommy - open the door." Suddenly, I nervously froze because here was the old girl nearly an entire day later. I knew Aunty was still mad and acting funny this morning, so something was definitely about to go down.

I quickly turned the water off, hopped down from the toilet and ran out of the bathroom door as I dried my hands off on my T-shirt. I stopped when I saw Aunty walk through the hallway in a fury. She looked as if at any moment she'd was getting ready to yank my mama's head right from her petite little body. I slowly crept down the hallway so that I could peep around the living room wall to watch as Aunty headed to open the wooden door.

"What you want?" Aunty barked as she stood in front of the metal cage door that kept burglars at bay.

"Oou girl hurry up and open up the door cause I got to pee bad," my mom said as she stood there shaking her legs while twisting on the door knob completely unaware of my aunty being pissed off. Unconcerned and more aggressively Aunty repeated it, "WHAT DO YOU WANT?"

I could barely see my mama through the screen on the metal door from the angle that I was standing, but I did see that she was still wearing the same clothes she wore yesterday. A black shirt that had the word 'Pretty' in silver text, some dingy light blue jeans with a pair of white Reebok classics and her hair looked a mess.

"Come on girl open the damn door," she said passive aggressively, thinking that my aunty was still joking around with her. Unbothered, my aunty stood there with her hand on the door knob watching as my mom paced back and forth in front of the door.

Slowly and reluctantly Aunty finally unlocked the door to let her in. Mama raced through the door saying, "Damn girl, it smells good in here. What you cook?" as she walked right by me in the hallway without even acknowledging me.

Running into the bathroom, she closed the door shut and hurried to use the toilet. She must've been holding it for as long as she was gone because it sounded as if she was pouring a gallon of water into the toilet. I turned around only to see that Aunty was now sitting at the dining room table staring off into space. Her left elbow was placed on the table with her hand resting underneath her chin as she the sound of her shaking right leg rattled the table.

Dramatically taking deep breaths, she began shaking her head as she rubbed her fingers across her forehead. But if she rocked that leg any harder, I promise you the pictures on the wall would've come crashing to the floor. The whole time I stood there watching her, I was I'm thinking to myself, "Let me go sit down because I know grown folks be tripping when they don't want kids in they business." So I went into the room pretending as if I was looking for something.

The toilet flushed, and for a few seconds, you could hear the sink running before mama opened the bathroom door. "Hey Ma," I said excitedly as she came out the bathroom. "Hey son," she replied in an aggravated tone as if I had done something wrong to her. I just stood there in the hallway confused because I didn't know what I did for mama to be upset with me.

Mama walked towards Aunty sitting at the dining table and was like, "Dang girl what you cook, fish and grits? It smells good up in here." Still shaking her leg, Aunty didn't respond to her. Mama realized that something was putting Aunty in a bad mood because of her body language, so she said, "Shay! What's wrong with you girl? You okay?" But once again Aunty didn't respond.

So, mama said, "Shay! Girl - I know you hear me, what's wrong with you?"

Aunty turned her head to the right, looked up at my mama and calmly said, "YOU GOT TO GO!" Shocked by what was just said, my mom tilted her head and said, "Huh? Got to go where, what you talking about?"

Growing more frustrated by the sight of my mom, Aunty became a little more aggressive with her words and replied, "If your ass can say 'Huh?' then you can hear. I said you got to go. Meaning you need to find somewhere else to stay cause you can't stay here no more."

Moms responded, "What in the hell are you talking about girl? Is this about the damn water bill? I told yo ass I was going to give you money for the water bill and cable today, so I don't even know why you are tripping," my mama continued, as she fumbled through her bra to grab the money she owed Aunty for the bills.

But that didn't seem to work because Aunty stood

up from the dining table and blurted out, "Trick you know ain't nobody talking about no god damn water bill money. Stop acting like you stupid. How the hell you gon' leave this damn boy in this house by his self all damn day. How dumb can you be? What if the god damn house would've caught on fire while he was in here sleeping? What the hell you was gon' do then? I swear you just about the dumbest damn person I've ever seen. Got me out here missing work and shit because of you," she shouted.

Before Aunty could even finish her rant, my mama yelled back, "Trick, I don't know who the hell you think you talking to, but you damn sure not talking to me. One, ain't nobody ask you to take off no damn work. You made that decision by your damn self.

"And two, Trick he's my damn son - I know how to take care of him. His ass ain't stupid, and he knows not to touch nothing that doesn't belong to him or do anything stupid while I am gone.

"Oou, girl let me calm down before I beat your ass in this house because you just got my blood running with this dumb shit. I know you done lost your rabbit ass mind talking to me like that. Trust me you got the wrong one baby girl."

Without warning, Aunty Shay ran up on my mama and SMACK! Slapped the crap out of her.

Caught by surprise mama yelled, "Trick! I know you ain't," and without finishing her sentence, they both began throwing hands with each other. The living room quickly filled with the sounds of chaos as they slammed into the wall, knocked over the glass coffee table while pulling on each other's hair and wildly throwing punches at one another.

When the fight broke out, I stood against the wall as an incredible sensation of disappointment gradually took over my body. I just knew this meant we were going to have to leave now. All she had to do was come back home last night I said to myself.

Standing on the wall tearing up, all I could do was scream out, "Mama! Mama! Stop! Aunty, No!"

The fight was about three minutes of them tussling with each other before they soon ran out of breath they laid on the floor holding on to each other's hair. They went back and forth telling one another to let go first until Aunty finally released my mama from her tight grip.

Aunty got up wheezing because she had bronchitis and said I'ma give you one hour to get y'all shit and get the hell out of my house, as she adjusted her bra back into position. Moms replied, "Trick don't even worry about it - we'll be out your shit and gone before then."

In sheer disappointment, my eyes flooded with tears as I watched over my mom's shoulder, while she hurried to pack all our belongings into two big black trash bags so that we could leave. I was going to try to tell Aunty that I love her before we left but she went into her room and closed the door on us.

I couldn't believe this was happening to us again. Out of all places, I was almost sure that this was going to be the one place we'd able to stay the longest until mama got on her feet again.

All packed up and ready; we headed outside with our bags in hand as we walked a few blocks over to the nearby corner store so that my mama could call somebody to come pick us up.

With the sun blazing and the clouds appearing to be on a lunch break, I was burning up on as we waited on the side of the road. It was crazy Miami hot out there. I thought man; she sure picked the wrong day for us to get kicked out. Sitting down on one of the bags of clothes I watched the cars pass by in front of me, hoping to get a gust of the cool wind they made riding down the street.

Using the pay phone on the side of the store, I could hear my mom fussing at someone about what just happened. Still hot and now sweating, I curiously wandered over inside of the convenient store. As I walked in, I saw a few people inside laughing as they were watching Jerry Springer on this small black television.

Of course, I didn't have any money. So I just wandered around the store picking up stuff, looking at the prices and placed them back down. I was going to ask my mama if she could give me a dollar but I knew, now wasn't the time to be asking her for anything because all she would've done was fussed, so I just said forget it.

It wasn't long before I made my way to the cooler section, where they had the quarter juices and fifty cent canned sodas. I popped open the door to the cooler, closed my eyes and just stood there allowing the cold air to hit my sweaty body. I must've been standing there gazing blankly for about three minutes when out of nowhere someone came up behind me and screamed, "BOO!" while slightly shaking my body as if they were about to push me into the cooler.

Stunned by what just happened, my heart instantly fell to my stomach as my body jerked forward. I quickly turned around to see who it was trying to scare me. It was this older cat from the neighborhood named Big Mike who watched out for me sometimes. He was the only dude who had this one gold front tooth and always wore cowboy hats and drove this beautiful long sleek baby blue Cadillac.

Laughing, Bike Mike said to me, "I scared you there didn't I boy? What are you doing over here in this refrigerator huh?" Still shaken, I softly said, "Nothing." He replied, "Ha-ha you a trip. I used to do the same thing sometimes. You were trying to cool off, weren't you?" Not wanting to get in trouble I lied and said, "No, I was just looking."

"Whoa, whoa come on now Youngblood you ain't got to lie to me man. You know I ain't here to get you in no trouble, come on now – you should know better than that. You have been my lil man since you were a baby.

Come on now, let's go buy you some candy or something, where your mama at?" He said before playfully grabbing me by the top of my head and closing the door to the cooler.

We sat there in the store for some time as he asked me how the ladies were treating me at school, if I still wanted to be an architect when I grew up and telling me to stay out of trouble. But what made Big Mike so cool, was that the fact that he was the only guy that ever talked to me about how to be a man, since I didn't have Pops to teach me.

I remember when he told me that, "Being a man ain't about how many women you got or how much jewelry you wear, it's about taking care of family and others; and by doing things for others from your heart without wanting anything in return." It was like he always knew what to say and when to say it.

Moments later, as we were sitting there talking, my mama came storming into the store. "Boy, what in the hell you doing in here and how the hell you just gon' leave our shit out there on the curb like nobody won't come up steal it?"

"Well, Hey to you too Red," Big Mike said to my mama sarcastically. "He was with me. I brought him in here to cool off and buy him something to eat."

"Well, he should've come and told me that," she replied to Bike Mike. "That's my fault Red, but you know he my main man, you know me and his daddy go way back."

But as soon as he brought up my dad, she gave him a disgusted look and grabbed me by the arm saying, "Well thank you, Mike, come on boy let's go."

"Hold on, hold on Red." Big Mike said as he paced behind us. "What Mike? What do you want? We got to go," my mama stated in a nasty voice.

"Calm down, calm down baby girl. Lil man left his drink that's all," then he kneeled in front of me and said, "Aye, you remember what I told you right?" I replied, "Yeah, I remember." Then he asked me. "So, what I told you?"

"You said that money doesn't make a man, a man makes money." Big Mike smiled and said, "My man," before dapping me up and sliding a twenty-dollar bill into my pocket.

"Okay, are you done?" my mom asked impatiently. "Yeah, we good Big Mike," said as he stood up. "Where y'all about to head? What you was doing washing clothes or something? You know could've called me up Red. I would've picked y'all up and dropped y'all back home when you were finished," Big Mike said to my mama even though I had already told him what happened. He just didn't want her to think he was being nosey or get mad at me for telling him what happened.

That's when this gold Lexus pulled up on the front street, and mama ordered me to get the bags. When I picked up one of the bags, this dude hopped out of the car yelling at my mama screaming, "Aye Yo! Let's go, man. Ain't nobody got all day to be waiting on your ass", then walked up to me, snatched the bag I had out of my hands and threw it in the back of the trunk.

"Okay - I'm coming," my mama replied in a submissive tone. I was thrown off because I was still trying to figure out who the hell he thought he was talking to because don't no man talk to my mama like that. My mama made her way over to the car and told me to get in. I put on my seat belt and looked out of the window as Big Mike made funny faces at me before we pulled off.

Slowly pulling off, I felt waves of sadness as we passed the street to my aunty house and I thought about us having to leave again. Suddenly, I heard, "Aye, Yo. You in the back seat." So, I looked up at the bald head and thin eyebrows staring at me through the rear-view mirror as he said, "Aye, whatever candy or chips you got back there with you. Don't be eating that shit in my car, you heard?"

CHAPTER 4

If You Only Knew

AFTER WE DIPPED from my aunty house, we started living at my mom's lil boyfriend house. I thought this was crazy because not once did I ever see this dude around and out of nowhere he just popped up into the picture. At first, she tried to lie to me by telling me that he was just one of her friends. But I wasn't stupid because why would male and female friends be sleeping in the same bedroom or taking showers together. Sometimes in the middle of the night when I would be sleeping on the couch in the living room I could hear her moaning as the bed simultaneously banged against the wall. Living there, I had to wake up and get ready for school by myself every day. My mama ain't have no car, so I would have to walk to school.

I would slowly get up from the couch – stretch out my arms and legs, sluggishly put the pillows back in place and begin folding my favorite power ranger sheet. I kept it through all the moves because it used to be Jaleel's and made me feel like a part of him was still here. Then I'd put it back next to my pile of clothes in the living room closet.

My mama was lazy, she ain't never cook me breakfast, in fact, she barely cooked at all. So, I had to wake up for school a little earlier this way I could get there on time for the free breakfast. Plus, I got to see and chill with some of my friends before school started. Somedays I would walk by the bedroom where my mama slept and peek to see if she was up. But she'd always be in the room sleep, wrapped up in the covers with her left one leg hanging out.

But Gary truly made me sick with all the slick shit he would do and say to me. In the mornings whenever I used to hear him walking through the living room prepping for work, I would lie on the couch pretending I was sleep until I heard him lock both doors as he'd be heading out to work.

Somedays I had to pee really bad but would just lay there as I'd listen to his footsteps walking back and forth through the house, his opening and closing the fridge, and even turning on the damn TV in the living room when he knew I was in there sleeping. But one thing that pissed me off the most was when he'd switch on the living room and kitchen lights while I was sleeping, then leave the house without turning them back off.

I always felt like he did all that stuff on purpose because he didn't care for me and since it was his house he could do whatever the hell he wanted, and I couldn't say anything about it. He was a first-class douche bag, and things like that just made me want to slap the shit out of him at times.

I remember this one time when he was supposed to give me a ride to school. This man came out into the living room, yanked my sheets off me talking about, "Aye, yo. Get up; your mama told me to take you to school, so get ready cause I'm about to leave and if you ain't ready when I'm about to hit, then your ass just going to get left."

The level of disrespect was unbelievable and demeaning. I woke up confused and wondering what in the heavens daylight would possess him to snatch the covers off me to wake me up. After that incident, I could care less about him taking me to school at that moment because I just wanted to punch him in the face for trying me like this.

With a slight mean mug, I got up aggressively, picked up my sheet from the floor and began fixing the pillows on the couch back in their right places. I was upset because this man was always testing my patience me and who knew I never wanted to go anywhere with him.

Whenever he would ask me "Aye, come ride with me to the store," I would always tell him, "Naw, I'm good I'ma stay home, I'm alright." After hearing that, he would catch an attitude and then say to my mama, "See what I'm talking about, every time I ask his ass if he want to go somewhere he always saying no but as soon as he needs somebody to drop him off to school he ain't got no problem with it. This that bullshit I be talking about."

As for my mom, it was almost as if like she had been brainwashed because nothing he did or said to me ever seemed to bother her the least bit. I couldn't understand how she would let anybody treat me the way he did and not say something about it. I was out here silently fighting this battle all by myself, hoping that one day my mama would rise to the occasion and address his ways.

But as time grew on us, so did the slander and mistreatment. It got to a point where he started calling me soft, saying that I wasn't a "real boy" because all I wanted to do was watch cartoons and stay in the house all day. He stated that, he ain't never seen no lil boy that always wanted to be in the house watching TV and trying to be up under his mama all day, as much as I did.

In his eyes, real boys went outside to play football, got in trouble for stealing shit and getting into fights with each other because that's what made them tough. I was convinced that for some reason - one I didn't quite understand, Gary was out to get me and ruin my life. At times, I couldn't believe that this grown man would make fun of me in front of his friends whenever they would come to his house and visit. All they would do is smoke weed and talk about who just went to jail or got shot.

Once, as I was sitting at the dinner table minding my own business, one of his friends asked, "Aye, what's up with your jit man? Why he ain't ever outside?" That's when Gary replied, "Man, that lil punk ain't my damn son. He a ole soft ass mama's boy that's why he ain't outside. All his ass ever do is sit in the damn house watching cartoons and playing with that damn notebook he got." Then he threw a used napkin at me and said, "Aye, why don't you take yo lil soft ass outside man? Ole nosey ass jit, I know you see real men in here talking."

Restraining every inch of muscle in my body from getting up and stabbing him right in the eye with this pencil clutched in my hand. I closed my notebook, got up and silently walked towards the door to I could go outside. As I walked past him in the living room he thought it would be comical to trip me, so he stuck his leg out causing me to stumble and fall. But in doing so, I ended up stabbing myself in the hand with the very pencil I wanted to use to gouge his eye out.

With a brief yelp from stabbing myself, I bounced up from the floor and began shaking my hand in pain. "Look what you made me do," I yelled out to him. But he didn't care; he just chuckled as he continued to smoke his blunt.

"Man take your ole soft ass outside and stop acting like a lil female before I beat you ass. That shit ain't going to kill you. I've been shot before and that ain't nothing close to what that shit felt like. I told y'all he was soft," he murmured to the other guys there.

For a moment, I just stood there in front of him, face balled up, eyes glossy from the tears building up due to the extreme amount of rage boiling inside of me. Then he leaned forward from his slouched position and said to me, "You know what it feels like to be shot? That shit burns like a mother boy. At first, you can't even feel that you've been shot, cause at the moment - the only thing that's on your mind is to 'survive.'

"So yo body become numb. You ain't worried no bullets hitting you, cause the only thing your mind is focused on, is getting the hell up out that situation. I'm telling you, you can't feel shit until after a few minutes later, once you finally get somewhere safe and you start seeing all that damn blood gushing out of your ass. Then out of nowhere, that shit hit you and start burning like a mother." He said to me wickedly.

Staring directly into his eyes, it felt as though everything in the room had been put on mute because I could only hear the thumping of my heartbeat, while I stood there contemplating if it would be a good idea for me to just go ahead and punch him right in his mouth.

Nothing would feel more satisfying than busting his lip wide open, but I knew I never had the chance because of how small I was compared to him. I was only about ninety pounds and knew that if I did attempt to swing at him, he might've tried to hurt me since my mama wasn't home really. So, I just picked up my notebook, walked to the front door and slamming it as hard as possible once I exited the house.

I left the house huffing and puffing looking at my hand as I headed down the sidewalk making my way to the neighborhood park. I sat down on top of a bench with my head in my lap crying, when I heard someone say to me, "Aye, you in my spot?" Still angry about my finger and thinking of what I would do to Gary if it weren't for my mama, I heard the voice again, "Aye, Yo! Wassup, you heard me? You sitting in my spot."

I looked up with my red, teary eyes only to see this skinny light brown kid standing in front of me. He then said, "Damn yo you look mad as shit, what happened to you?" But I wasn't in the mood to talk to anyone, so I responded, "Nothing" as I lowered my head down in-between my legs.

He responded, "Well shit - what happened to your hand? That dang sure look like something happened to it. It looks like somebody stabbed you in the hand with a pencil or something." That's when I replied, "Leave me alone man," as I kept my head slumped between my legs.

For some reason, the kid decided to come over and sit next to me on the bench. "Let me see," he said, gazing at my hand dripping with blood. "Damn yo, that cut looks deep boy. I know that crap got to hurt, why you ain't put no band aid over that?"

I looked over at him sideways before attempting to

hide my hand under my and responded, "If I had a band aid don't you think I would've put one over it?" before I shifted to the left of the bench, trying to create some space between the two of us.

"Aye fool, all I'm saying is that thing looks bad, and you should cover it up before it gets infected. You ain't got to be getting mad at me. I ain't do nothing to you," he said. "What want? I don't even know you," I replied as I became annoyed with him.

"I don't know you either, I was here first, and when I came back, all I know is you were sitting in my spot on the bench. I was just going to tell you to move, but then I heard you crying, so I just came to see if you were straight. You tripping."

Still, I remained quiet as he leaned lower to try and look at my face asking again, "Yo everything good? I ain't never seen a dude bleeding and crying like this out in public. That ain't a good look. Especially, not over here in this hood. You got to tighten up."

Agitated, I replied to him, "I said, I'm good man." But for some reason he didn't believe me, so he said, "Bruh, if you ain't mad, then what you out here looking like you pissed off at the world for? That don't make any sense. You don't see this beautiful ass sun shining or hear these birds chirping? Slightly nudging my right shoulder," he then said, "Come on now, you ain't got to tell me if you don't want to but I know you ain't crying for nothing."

on the bench. "You - You just wouldn't understand man. Even if I told you what I was mad about," I said, before stepping off the bench and moving over to another one.

But instead of leaving me alone, like a fly he ended up following me over to the other bench. Taking another stab at getting the conversation he said, "You know what? Honestly, I just think you scared to say what's on your mind cause you soft and think that I'm going to tell somebody. I barely even know you man, Who I'm going to tell?"

Turning around infuriated by him calling me soft I replied, "I ain't soft and exactly - You don't even know me, so stay out my business before we have a problem." Pulling a white paper napkin out of his pocket he said, "Man, here. Take this napkin and shut up because you sound stupid. Wrap it around your that finger so you can stop all that blood from leaking everywhere."

I reached out and snatched the napkin from his hand, that's when he propped his leg on the park bench to tie his shoe lace. "But seriously though man, I ain't trying to be nosey he said. Shoot, I am going through my own problems at home. That's the only reason why I even come out here to the park," he said to me.

Folding the napkin so that I could wrap it around my finger, I listened as he continued talking, "It ain't nothing wrong with crying man. I cry all the time, especially when my punk as step dad be trying me and shit. When he said that, I looked over at him kind of surprised because I didn't expect him to be going through something similar to what I was going through.

I remained skeptical of him because I had never seen him around here before, so I braced myself in case he trying to rob me or something. I knew that sometimes when guys were trying to get into gangs, they would take other people shoes or just beat up random people to get initiated, so I had to be on standby.

Plus, I didn't feel comfortable with telling a stranger my business about what was going on with me at home, even though it was clear that we had something in common. So, as he continued to talk, I just sat there and listened to him as he began explaining to me what being at home was like for him.

"Well since you don't want to tell me what's up with you, I'll tell you what's up with me. So how about, I was home minding my own business. Having an absolutely fine day, until my mama boyfriend walked into my room and started messing with me, trying to make me feel like I was less of a person than he was. He kept calling me out of my name, making me upset to the point that I felt like killing his ass. So instead of doing that, I just got up and left the house. I walked out here so that I could cool off and relax my mind, this way I could save myself from doing something stupid that would probably make the call the police on me.

"I swear - it's like this dude always got something to

say to me man. I could be sitting there doing everything I was told, and somehow, he always finds something negative to say about me. At times, I find myself thinking about all the cruel things that I would do to him if I ain't have no common sense. But then, I realize how much I don't want to go to jail and especially how lucky he was that he was with my mama, cause if it wasn't for her - ain't no telling what I'd do to his milk dud head ass."

Although I was pretending to be aloof and not to pay him much attention, I couldn't help but be shocked that he brought up the same exact topic that forced me to come out here myself. And without even noticing it I replied, "I know that you mean," causing him to respond by jokingly shoving me and saying, "Oh, so now you want to say something? Man, you don't even know what I'm talking about."

I lifted my finger in the air and said, "Well how the hell you think I got this? You think I just went ahead and stabbed myself? Man, my mama ole punk ass boyfriend made me fall and stab myself in the hand with a pencil. I swear I wanted to knock his head clean off his shoulders in that house. I promise you boy, one of these days I'ma end up going to jail for killing his ass if he keeps on trying me. I'm tired of him messing with me for no reason and calling me soft."

Staring at me with his eyes stretched wide he said to me, "Yo, that's wild." I turned and replied, "See - I told you, I know exactly how you feel man." He looked towards the ground and then back up at me before dramatically saying, "Yo, you got the same problems I got going on at home, that's crazy." Shaking his head in disbelief, he followed up with, "See man; something told me to come over here to see what was wrong with you and look at that, we both over going through the same dang problem."

Sucking his teeth, he uttered, "Man I swear I don't know what be going through these dude's heads with the way they think they can just talk to us any way that they feel like. But you know what's crazy and make matters worse?" He asked. "Naw, what's that?" I replied. "It's like whenever I try to talk to my mama about what her boyfriend be saying to me and how he makes me feel, it's like she almost instantly shuts me down. Taking his side, by trying to tell me, I need to stop over exaggerating or that he ain't trying to hurt me, he just be playing.

"That don't make no sense to me though. Like, what kind of grown man plays all the time by picking on lil kids all day and making them feel bad? This dude is supposed to be showing me how to be a man and teaching me what not to do in life, but all he ever does is say slick and hurtful stuff to me.

"What breaks my heart is that with my mama bro - I feel like she doesn't even care about what I go through anymore. I ain't trying to say that I hate her or nothing because after all, she is my mama. But boy, I promise I can't stand her ass sometimes man. It just feels like, ever since this dude came into the picture, he ruined the whole relationship that she and I had with each other.

"You know what I'm saying? He said, looking over at me with his eyes filled with water. I could see the frustration in his glossy eyes, as he attempted to hold back his tears. Then he looked down at the dirt he was kicking before placing his head on his lap to cry.

For a moment I thought to myself, "Here I am, holding my guard up, being selfishly rude, when this kid honestly came over here to see if he could help me." Starting to feel guilty as he sat next to me crying I placed my left hand on his shoulder and told him.

"Aye man, you ain't got to cry, everything going to be straight. We all got to deal with bullshit growing up around here, and I know you been through worse. You just go to ignore him that's all.

"I just think that sometimes, people who don't understand us, try to make themselves feel bigger than us by saying hurtful things to get under our skin. But it's going to get better. You just got to keep you head up bruh.

"I know for me - I got a bad temper, so when stuff like this happens I just try to leave the house or go somewhere to calm down because I know if I don't, something bad going to happen. So, don't worry about it man, in a few years you can move out and not have to deal with him ever again."

Feeling encouraged by what I just said, He slowly lifted his head, wiped away his tears while slightly smiling and said, "You know what? You right man. In a few years, I'll be out of there, and they won't ever have to worry about me again. But for now, I just got to keep my head up and hope that one day, things will start to get better.

"I just get tired of dealing with it sometimes, so I let it get to me. I'ma try to find different ways to deal with they nonsense." I then replied, "Trust me, that's all you got to do," with the intentions of giving him hope that his ideas will work.

The interesting thing about this was that here I was telling him how to go about handling things when I struggled with trying to figure out how to deal with stuff myself. That's when, he sat up and said, "Thanks, man. I needed that but what's your name?" he laughed after realizing, we'd been sitting here the whole time chopping it up and didn't even know each other's name. "Dang you right," I said, "But name DJ. What's your name?" That's when he responded, "My name Chad."

Shortly after, Chad then asked, "How old are you, DJ? Like thirteen?" I replied, "Naw, I'm twelve right now, but I'll be thirteen in a few months, how about you?" I asked. "I'm twelve too," he said, "My birthday coming up soon but I don't even know if I care anymore." Confused by his comment, I asked: "What you mean by that?"

"Cause man, it's just like life ain't fun no more to me. Like, I am trying to do good in school and all that other stuff so that my mama can be proud of me, but it seems she doesn't even care. I do my best to stay out of trouble, but somehow none of that even matters because now this dude is up here at home trying to pick on me just because I don't like to do the things he thinks I should be doing.

"He might call me soft, but in all honesty, I'm just a pretty boy," Chad said to me causing me to laugh. "Naw, I'm serious," he said, "See, I just like to chill, look fresh and try to get at all these fine girls at the school, you feel me? I can't be out here playing in this dang hot ole sun all day. I got to take care of my sexy face," he said while pretending to play with the invisible hair on his bare chin. "You know, I got to look good for the ladies cause they be after a player," Chad said humorously.

The both of us sat on that bench for nearly three hours discussing almost everything we had gone through. Learning so much about each other, we find out that we had a whole lot more in common than we expected. With his caramel complexion, skinny little chicken legs, and silky wavy black hair, I assumed that he was a bit more privileged and didn't have the same problems as I did.

Meeting Chad gave me a feeling of relief on the inside. Even though it was kind of strange how we met, I felt like I finally had somebody that I could relate to and possibly talk to whenever things got rough at home. Being out there so long we lost track of time, but once the street lights flickered on and the sky began to turn dark orange, we knew that it was time for us to head back home.

A police officer had pulled up on us at the park and said that it was getting too late and we couldn't be out here at the park any longer. So, we dapped each other up and headed our separate ways, until next time.

Walking back home, I felt reenergized and ready to take on life again. My mind was clear, and I was feeling hopeful that things would get better at home if I kept a positive attitude. I knew I couldn't continue to let Gary get under my skin. So, instead of showing that I was mad, I was just going to stay out of his way and kill him with kindness whenever he attempted to disrespect me. This way his lil ugly ass would never have anything to say to me.

Once I got home, I walked to my mama room to see if she was back home from work. She wasn't in the room, but I saw that her work uniform shirt and work shoes were laying on the floor which meant she was either in the kitchen or using the bathroom. Happy that Gary had left, I headed into the living room to watch TV. I appreciated when he was gone because I got alone time and I could bother my mama without him being present.

Thirsty as I waited for my mom to finish up in the bathroom, I headed to the kitchen to grab something to drink. We had a half full pitcher of red Kool-Aid left in in the fridge, so I pulled it out and tilted the pitcher over my head pouring a nice gulp of it down my dry throat. I only did this when no one was looking, so that I didn't have to use a cup and be forced to wash some dishes that I ain't use. In the distance, I heard the toilet flush, so I quickly placed the Kool-Aid pitcher back into the fridge and walked out the kitchen like nothing ever happened.

Moms walked out of the bathroom with just a bra and her black work pants on when I said, "Hey Ma!" She replied in a halfhearted tone, "Hey!" Running up behind her as she entered the bedroom, I attempted to hug and tickle her but she pushed me aside saying, "Move boy, I'm not in the mood stop playing."

Only trying to show her some affection, I continued to joke around but again she insisted I stopped playing when she turned around and gave a serious look that suggested she'd smack me if I didn't.

I stopped tickling her, and as she climbed onto the bed, I kneeled next to the bed and placed my arms on her legs as she positioned herself underneath the sheets. I asked, "How was work? You brought me back some apple pies today?" She replied exhaustedly, "It was the same as usual. Can't you see I'm trying to go to sleep, go in the living room or something."

I responded, "I know - I just missed you that's all ma. I just wanted to see how you were doing today." But as usual, she just ignored me and turned away with her butt pointing towards my face. I leaned in and laid my head on her butt as I rubbed her legs and said, "Ma - you know I love you right?" while glancing at the TV playing Sanford and son.

"Yeah, Yeah, I love you too," she replied before swiping at my head and telling me, "Go on now. I know you heard me say I was trying to go to sleep? Get off me and go in the living room, don't make me tell you again."

Saddened, I picked my head up, but before leaving I gently kissed the skin of her cold exposed arm. Then I headed back into the living room, grabbed my blanket out of the closet, turned on the TV and moved the pillows out the way so that I could lay down comfortably before falling asleep.

CHAPTER 5

Being Down

A BRISK TUESDAY afternoon during Christmas break of my first year in high school. The wind blew a chilly breeze of cold air that made your face feel as though it was seconds from turning into ice. I was now in the ninth grade and felt like I knew what it took to be a man. Having a nonchalant attitude towards everything, never actually speaking to anyone unless I knew them and just overall laidback, no one gave me problems. Although I wasn't like the spoiled hood rich kids that couldn't live a day without wearing name brand clothes, I still wore all the new Jordan's and tried to keep myself looking decent times. I guess that's why people used to like me because they thought I had a nice wardrobe. At this point in my life, I was practically raising myself because my mama had stopped giving me money a long time ago, so I had to get by any means to get the things I wanted

Forced to be on the streets trying to prove to Gary that I wasn't soft, I started getting into a lot of trouble at school. I wasn't bringing guns, selling drugs or getting into fights all the time. I just had a slick mouth that got me into a lot of trouble because whenever a teacher would say something to me that I ain't like, I would respond with whatever was on my mind at that time.

Hanging with my homies from the hood, I picked up some bad habits. I was getting caught skipping class, trying to sneak out of the school and even gambling in the school bathrooms. It all caught up to me one day when my mama got off work early and came to the school looking for me, but I was nowhere to be found.

The school administrators looked at the video from the surveillance cameras, and it showed me along with three other guys jumping a fence during the lunch hour. When I got home that day, I didn't make it past the living room before my mama came up to me and started busting me upside my head.

Now almost the same height as her, I just ate the punches and dealt with them because I ain't care no more about her trying to beat me. Our relationship had gotten so bad, that we barely spoke to each other. Besides, when I used to do good in school, she didn't care about me then, so why should I care now.

After getting in trouble a few more times, my grandma Diana who was my dad's mom asked if I could stay with her for winter break so that she'd be able to spend some time with me. She was hoping that by being around her, she would be able to steer me onto the right path.

At first, when the idea was brought up I didn't want to go because I ain't want to spend my winter break listening to no old lady trying to tell me what I needed to be doing. But once I got over to her house, things were a whole lot different than what I imagined.

Every morning of that winter break I woke up to the smell of butter biscuits baking in the oven, salmon croquettes frying on the stove and grits so hot that they nearly burned a hole through my tongue. Grandma Dee is what we called her as a nickname. She and my older cousin Aaliyah - who we called Liyah, lived together in this nice three-bedroom house over off on Eighty-Fifth Street and Twelfth Avenue.

Grandma Dee had gotten full custody of Liyah when she was just a child because Liyah mama, who was my grandma Dee's younger sister, was on drugs and couldn't take care of Liyah. So, she raised her as one of her kids. Knowing that about Grandma Dee, I gained a higher level of respect for her.

But just being around them made me feel good because they treated me like the human person I was. I remember once when I gave Liyah an attitude about moving my clothes because she had folded them and put them away, it was the first time she snapped on me and the moment I realized how much they cared about me.

I had left some clothes out in the room, and when I searched for them, I gave her an attitude when I asked where she put my stuff. Feeling disrespected she said to me, "Boy, I don't know where you come from having an attitude with somebody because they helped you out but you better act like you got some sense and say, 'Thank You.' Ain't nobody your maid, so you better be grateful that I even did that." Before storming off, angered that I had the audacity to question her about folding my clothes.

Later, that day when she was in the kitchen washing the dishes after Grandma Dee had finished serving dinner. I eased my way into the kitchen and stood next to her. "Don't worry Liyah; I'll wash the dishes for you," I said softly." I ain't know how to tell people sorry, so to me, this was my way of giving her an apology. That's when she said, "Oh so you think that by washing the dishes for me, I'm just supposed to change my mind about being mad at you? Ha - you must be crazier than I thought."

Hearing her say that to me, kind of hurt my feelings on top of the fact that she just straight up rejected my attempt of an apology. So, I put my head down and slowly turning away when she said to me, "Boy, if you don't pick your head up and get back over here. I'm just messing with you. Come help me put these dishes in the cabinet." Quickly turning around, pretending to frown, she smiled at me while she stood there scrubbing out an empty pan of mac n cheese.

Walking back over, I grabbed some of the clean dishes and began to place them in the cabinets. Liyah said to me, "Now the next time you disrespect me like that after I did something to help your ill ugly butt out, we going to fight."

Laughing at her statement, I kneeled to put the big stainless-steel rice pot back into the cabinet space below. I then said, "Naw Liyah, you don't want to see me in a fight. My hands too quick." She responded, "That's fine, you can have quick hands all you want but I'ma still beat you lil popcorn head ass you if try me like that again," before we both burst into laughter.

"I know you ain't used to having people do stuff for you. I just wanted you to know that you got to be aware of what you say, as well as, how you treat people." Understanding where she was coming from, I replied, "I feel you," as we continued putting the dishes away.

Once finished we finished and after drying our hands, she then came over to hug me. In a serious tone, while pointing her finger in my face, she said, "You are my lil cousin, and I love you, but I promise you try me like that again. Trust me, I'ma slap that lil watermelon head of yours clean off your shoulders."

Time was flying as Christmas Eve snuck up on us. Grandma Dee was having a Christmas Eve party at her house, and out nowhere a whole bunch of family members that I'd never met started showing up. Every time Grandma Dee would introduce me to one of them, the first thing they would say was, "Well I'll be damned Dee. If this goddamn boy don't look just like his damn daddy! Damn Derrick got some strong ass genes," or they'd say to me, "Boy you look just like yo daddy. If he was here, he couldn't deny your ass even if he wanted to."

I was getting annoyed by them telling me how much I looked like my daddy, but I also thought these folks were hilarious. The thing that I liked about this side of the family the most was that none of them seemed to be judging me or making me feel like I had to prove something to them. They were just excited to see me and happy that I was around because they hadn't seen me since my father passed away.

The house was filled with love and laughter, as some of the older folks sat at the dinner table playing spades. I was sitting on the couch trying to stay awake because I had caught the iitis, as my grandma watched one of them boring old Christmas movies on TV.

That's when my cousin Bam came strutting through the door, way after everyone finished eating and there was barely any food left. He was wearing this big ole gold chain, a gold Cuban link bracelet, long white T-shirt with red shorts and rocking some all-white tennis shoes.

When he came in, he greeted all the adults in the room first before he turned around towards me and shouted out, "Aye grandma, who jit this is? He looks familiar."

She replied, "That's your uncle Derrick baby boy."

"Baby? Man, this lil ugly dude ain't no baby," he said before coming up to play fight with me. Then he asked, "What's your name again lil homie?" Smiling as I held my fist up, anticipating him to start throwing fake jabs again, I said, "My name DJ! Why - what's up?" In my tough voice.

Bam looked at me and said, "DJ? Man, bring yo lil skinny butt here," as he picked me up in the air and threw me over his shoulder. "Now what's up lil chump?" He uttered, while I playfully hitting him in the side to let me down as he spun me around in the living room.

"Alright, Alright, Okay Bam, put the boy down. Can't you see people in here trying to watch TV?" Grandma Dee yelled out. She was the only one truly zoned in watching that boring movie, but out of respect, he placed me back onto the couch and sat next to me.

Slouching back, he slapped me on the chest and said, "How old are you now DJ?" Energized, I replied, "I'm fifteen." Rubbing his chin Bam said, "Fifteen? Dang boy - time flying by like a mud. I remember when you were just a lil baby stinking up the house with yo shitty ass pampers."

"Bam! You better watch your mouth over there," Grandma blurted out. "Oh, yea my bad grandma, I ain't mean to say that," Bam replied. "So, what school you go to?" Bam asked me. With pride, I said, "I got to Da West!"

"Oh, you go to Da West? That's what's up," Bam replied. "Yeah, this my first year out there," I added. "That's what's up lil homie," he said. "I used to go out there too, but I had to drop out though. I wasn't making any money wasting all that time in school learning about bullshit I was never going to use in real life no way. Plus, I ain't never really like school anyway, you feel me? That shit just wasn't for me."

"Bam, If I tell you one more time to watch your mouth, I'ma come over there and slap you in it," Grandma Dee said as a final warning to Bam. "My fault grandma, I'ma stop cussing for real this time. That just slipped out," he replied to Grandma. "Alright now, I'm not playing with you," she said while rolling her eyes before continuing to watch her movie.

"What's your favorite subject he asked me?" Shrugging my shoulders, I told him, "I don't know." Baffled, he asked, "Man how you don't know what your favorite subject is? Even I had a favorite subject in school, even though I barely went to school."

"I mean, I don't be caring about school like that. I just go cause my mama make me," I said trying to impress him. Hoping that by making it seem as if I could care less about school he'd think I was cool. But, my statement did have some truth to it because over time I had lost interest in school since my mama never really pressed me about it.

That's when Bam hit me in the chest again and told me, "Aye, come go outside with me real quick." Eager to go outside with him, I hopped of the couch and followed him to the door but before we could exit Grandma Dee yelled out,

"Nun Uh. Where is y'all going? No...Bam, you ain't finna take him nowhere with you."

"Naw grandma, we ain't going nowhere. We just finna be right here outside in the front yard. See, I can't even go nowhere Uncle Rod already done blocked my car in," he said while pointing out the window at his red Mustang.

"Alright now Bam, don't make me come out there looking for y'all or it's going to be some trouble," she said to him still skeptical of his intentions.

Placing his hand on the top of my head, moving me towards the open door he said, "Come on now grandma - we ain't going nowhere, I promise. We going to be right there by my car." Walking outside, I said, "So, where are we going?" Believing that he was lying to grandma just so that she would leave us alone. But looking straight ahead at his car, he smiled and said, "Dang boy - you sure ask a lot of questions, huh?"

Not trying to be a bug, I instantly dropped the subject, followed behind him quietly as we walked out of the gate and up to his car. Approaching the car, he clicked the button to unlock the door, which made a chirping sound, as he told me to hop in on the passenger side. He then turned the car on, and my initial reaction was, "Man

- this dude bout to get us in trouble," and just like I figured, grandma came busting through the front door with her hand on her hip frowning her face.

Bam opened his door, stretching his left leg out onto the ground as he stood up and yelled out, "Grandma we ain't going nowhere. I just turned the car on so we can get some heat. It's cold out here," She stood there doubtfully and pointed her finger at him, signally that if he dared leaving with me, he was going to be in a whole heap of trouble. Then she slowly turned away and went back inside of the house.

Ducking back into his seat, Bam slammed the door shortly and said irritably, "Damn man - grandma be tripping sometimes. She acting like I ain't hear her the first time she told us not to leave," as he reached into the armrest of the car and pulled out a small container of cinnamon. Staring at him, I tried to figure, what in the hell was he doing with a container of cinnamon in his armrest?

He then said to me, "Aye lil homie, you smoke?" Not wanting to appear like a buster, I replied, "Yeah, I smoke sometimes." Looking at me unconvinced, he asked, "Since when?" Smiling I said, "Since like middle school, my homies and I from my block used to jump the gate during lunch and go to one of my homies granddaddy crib to smoke."

I was obviously telling the truth about skipping school but the smoking part, now I knew damn well that part wasn't true. I ain't want to look soft in front of Bam, so I had to exaggerate my story. To be honest, I hated the smell of weed because it reminded me of Gary. He smoked that shit inside the house all day, to the point that I would get headaches from inhaling the secondhand smoke.

Looking at Bams' face, I could tell he didn't care if I was telling the truth or not. He didn't even bother to respond to my story, as he took out one of his pre-rolled blunts and sparked it up. Taking a deep puff, he blew out a huge cloud of smoke and asked me, "You want to take a hit?"

Briefly pausing, I looked over at him not knowing if should say yes or no. Then he laughed before he took another hit saying, "I thought you told me you smoked lil homie?" Stuttering over my words I replied, "Yeah, yeah like I do - I do smoke sometimes, but I just don't smoke all the time."

Again, he laughed before saying, "Aye look man, you ain't got to lie to me lil homie. I probably started smoking way after the age you at now, so it's cool if you don't smoke man." Hearing Bam tell this to me, there was a great feeling of relief that traveled through my body. I attempted to laugh it off by saying, "Naw like for real though I do be smoking. I just don't be feeling like smoking sometimes cause it be giving me headaches."

"Yeah, yeah - whatever you say lil homie," he said while turning up this old school Trick Daddy song playing as we sat in the car. "Aye, what you be doing after school?" he asked me. Curious to know why he asked me this, I suspiciously replied, "Uh, nothing. I just go straight home or chilling with my homies in the hood sometimes. Why, what's up?" Slowly he replied, "I want you to start kicking it with me after school. Let me show you how to get these females and how to put some bread in your pocket. I know you ain't got no job," he said to me.

Not knowing exactly what he was referring to about putting bread in my pocket. I was hesitant as I responded, "For sho - that sounds like a plan to me." He then said, "My man," as he reached his fist over to pound me up. "I knew you were an alright jit DJ. What time you be getting out of school?" he asked. Reluctantly I told him, "I be getting out of school like one-thirty to two o'clock."

"Aight then lil homie, I'ma start picking you up after school, so you can ride with me and learn how to put this bread in your pocket. That's straight with you?" he asked. Thinking about all the reasons why this didn't seem like a good idea and having a gut feeling that going with him after school wouldn't be the brightest idea, I went ahead anyway and replied, "Yeah, that's good with me."

We sat in the car for about another twelve minutes or so as he smoked the last of his blunt, while I inhaled that second-hand smoke. He eventually turned the car off and started letting the windows down. "Yeah boy, we got to let this thang air out before we go back in there. That's that loud I'm smoking on, so I know grandma will have a fit if we went back in there smelling too dank. She don't be tripping when she can smell it just a lil bit but if it's too dank, oh yeah, she gon' have a heart attack in that house and I ain't trying to hear her mouth no more today boy."

I laughed as he asked me to grab a bottle of cologne that was stashed in the glove compartment. When I opened it, I saw that he had a gun resting right next to the bottle of cologne. He then said, "Spray some all over your body, then hand it to me so I can use it before we go back in lil homie."

After we had stepped out of the car and towards the house he stopped me and said, "Aye look, don't tell nobody that I'ma be picking you up from school now. This going to be just between you and me, you heard me?"

Staring at him even more regretful than before that I agreed to let him pick me up I replied, "Don't worry, I got you." He looked at me intensely as if he was staring into my soul and said, "I'm serious now. I don't want to hear nobody saying that they heard you say something to somebody else or told them about anything we discussed." To reassure Bam, I continued by confidently saying, "Trust me, I got you Bam. This just between you and me."

When we got back inside, my nerves were bad because I felt like I had just made a bad deal. Even though Bam was family, still, I barely knew him enough to know anything about what he did or who he was exactly. All I knew, was that his name was Bam and he was my cousin. I guess I was just so caught up with being impressed by how much gold he was wearing; it never dawned on me to figure out how exactly did Bam get his money.

On top of being nervous about kicking it with Bam, I became extra paranoid once we entered the house because the intake from the secondhand smoke of Bams' loud weed had me feeling dizzy. I felt as though, everybody was looking at me because they smelled weed on us, as I sat back down to watch the TV.

It didn't take long before the sensation of paranoia set in, and I fell asleep on the couch. Somewhere around nine o'clock, Liyah came out into the living and woke me up. I slowly crept up, wiping the slob from the side of my face, as I noticed that everybody else had left. Liyah said to me in an intense whisper, "DJ! Wake up!" I replied, "I'm up, what's up Liyah?"

She then said to me with the seriousness of her face and the sound of concern in her voice, "DJ, listen to me." Still disoriented and trying to wake myself up, while feeling somewhat light headed, I replied, "Huh?" Liyah then firmly placed her hand on my chin and tilted my head back slightly squeezing my cheeks together. "DJ, I do not want you hanging around Bam, do you hear me?" Staring at her with my bloodshot red and droopy eyes, I sluggishly said, "Huh? What's wrong with Bam, Liyah? Bam cool."

With a deep sigh of disapproval and squatting as she gently bounced on her tippy toes to get closer to me, she responded, "Listen to me, DJ. Bam is not somebody I want you to be hanging around, you understand me? He maybe our blood but that doesn't mean anything. I'm telling you now; all Bam do is worry about Bam. He ain't going to do nothing but bring trouble around your way, so you better stay away from him. You are better than he is - smarter than he is – a whole lot more handsome. So, all I'm asking is for you to do me a favor and think twice before you decide to get into another car or go anywhere with him again."

Being so high, I could barely respond because I was more focused on trying to stop my head from spinning. Noticing it herself, she sucked her teeth before putting my arm around her neck as we walked towards the bathroom so she could have me take a shower. Softly whispering to herself, she said, "Ass better be happy grandma ain't notice y'all was high or else she would have kicked both of y'all asses."

Hearing that and with the little energy I had, I managed to mumble, "But I wasn't smoking Liyah I was just sitting in the car." She replied, "It doesn't matter if you were smoking or not, you were in the car and now you high." Sitting me on the toilet, she said, "Take off your clothes but leave your boxers on," as she turned on the bath water to run me a warm shower.

She then handed me a glass of cold water, that I gulped down so fast you would've thought I had been stranded on a desert island. "Thank you Liyah; I needed that," I said, as she stood next to me with her hands on her hips watching me clumsily take off my shirt. "Boy I tell you if it ain't one thing with you, it's another," she said before walking out the bathroom as I took my pants off.

CHAPTER 6

Let Me Be Great

"HEY, MA! YOU think I can hold twenty dollars so that I can buy lunch at school this week. I promise you I'ma give it back to you as soon as I get it." The task of asking my mama for something was almost like applying for food stamps. She'd always have a million and one questions about what I was going to do with the money, or she'd start fussing about how I must think money grew on trees. Most of the times I would've preferred either a simple 'Yay' or 'Nay' before going on about my business with whatever decision she made. Things were getting a lot tighter around the house now that she had just given birth to a baby by this sucker Gary, something that I still couldn't believe.

With the baby around now, it was almost as if I had become a figment of their imagination. It seemed like no one heard anything I said, cared about my feelings or even noticed I was there. I just kind of felt alone but once we finally moved into this two-bedroom duplex where I had my own room. I sort just did the same thing to them that they'd been doing to me by locking myself in my room only leaving out when I got hungry, I had to go to school or do something else I thought was important.

Sometimes I'd catch myself, looking into the mirror, just wondering, "Why am I even here? What was my purpose for being here when nobody in this damn house seemed to appreciate all the good in my heart that I once had to offer?" The nights felt longer and the days shorter as I struggled to stay asleep. I'd often wake up in the middle of the night and just stare into the darkness, wondering if there was anything good that could come out of my life.

My little brother was about the only thing that gave me hope during these moments of doubt. His soul was precious soul; his eyes glistened as though they were the stars themselves. I couldn't blame him for how they made me feel, after all, he was just a baby. But when I would look into his small googly eyes, I'd always wonder, "What was it that he saw in me?"

Apart of me was jealous that he was going to have everything that I ever wanted. He was going to have both of his parents, undivided attention and the feeling of being loved unconditionally by someone you loved. But there I was, sectioned off in my lonesome, left on my own to discover my path in this harsh world of mine. I never really had a stable male role model but being very observant, I watched how dudes that lived in my community moved and went about handling things.

I know that Liyah told me she didn't want me being around Bam. But one day when school was out I was standing out front talking with this girl I knew when I saw Bams' car parked across the street. I knew it was his Mustang because I remembered the Miami Heat license plate he had on the front of his car. He was a few months late since he had told me he was going to start picking. So, after the third day when he didn't show up, I just figured he must've realized I wasn't that cool after all.

It shocked me when I saw that he was outside waiting for me. Being the character that he was, Bam hung himself halfway through the driver's side window of his car screaming my name.

"Aye yo, DJ! Aye DJ!", He screamed out to get my attention. Talking with this girl I knew, she began laughing when Bam started obnoxiously honking the horn. She asked me, "You know who that is calling you?" Embarrassed, I replied, "Yeah, I know who that is. I'll holla at you later," before giving her a hug and walking away.

Heading to Bams' car, I smiled the whole way over because although I was shocked he was here, I was also happy that he finally came through. When I approached him, I said, "Well dang, Bruh. It's about time you came and picked me up."

"Man, don't even try me like that lil homie," Bam said as he reached out to dap me up. "I just got caught up with something that's all. I needed to stay low-key for a minute, you feel me?"

"Naw, it's all good Bam. I was just messing with you," I responded. That's when he said, "Man get your lil uglass in the car so we can ride out." Laughing at his comment, I hurried around the front of the car and hopped into the passenger seat. As soon as I got in, Bam mashed on the gas, causing the tires to squeal as we peeled out from in front of the school.

I swear this man ain't care about no speed, as we hit a hard right at the stop light to head across Twelfth Avenue Bridge. Holding onto the door handle, my body swung to the left as I struggled to keep myself from sliding out of the seat. He had to be going at least seventy miles per hour, on that bridge, flying right through a red light.

I could feel the pressure of the hot wind press against my face as we flew down the street before slowing down at a red light. Once we stopped, Bam asked me, "Aye, you ate yet?" I replied, "Yeah, I had a slice of pizza today, but that was about it." He the responded sarcastically, "A slice of pizza? Man, that ain't no real food. You eat conch?"

Excited, I looked over at Bam and replied, "Heck yeah I eat conch. Who doesn't eat conch? Shoot If I could

I'd eat conch and shrimp all day if I had the money." He laughed at me and said, "Me too lil homie. Well shit, aight then, let's go get some conch and shrimp from Shulers." Little did he know but Shulers' was my favorite seafood restaurant and hearing him say that just made my day even better.

Smiling and looking ahead, I saw that the light was getting ready to turn green, so without hesitation I hurried to fastened my seatbelt because the way this dude was driving, I was liable to fly out of the window.

It took us about seven minutes on the road before we finally pulled up to Shulers' parking lot. When we walked into the restaurant, the people inside greeted us with open arms. The older guy behind the counter taking food orders said, "Hey there Bam – where you been at man? We ain't seen you up here in a lil minute? What, your girlfriend had you locked up in the dog house?" Bam responded with a laugh saying, "Haha you a trip but naw, I just been busy. I came up here to get my lil soldier and me something to eat before we head out."

"Oh okay, that's good to hear. Glad you alright," the guy said. "Well gone ahead and order then, it's on the house man." Bam responded, "Aye, on the real though. This why I mess with y'all man. Y'all stay looking out for a brother." The older guy shook his head and said, "As always, you know we got to make sure we keep our loyal customers happy."

After Bam ordered, the guy then looked over at me

and said, "What's up young blood? What you getting?" Once our food was ready, the both of us went outside to eat by Bams' car. I tell you that conch was everything. Golden brown, tender, and flaky as I drenched it with lime juice and ketchup. Bam joked about how fast I was eating by saying, "Dang lil homie slow down. The food already dead man. It ain't going nowhere," as he laughed before playfully sticking his fork in my plate and taking a small piece of conch.

"So, Bam," I said to him. "Wassup lil homie?" he replied. "Like I ain't trying to be nosey or nothing but can I ask you something?" Tilting his head sideways to look at, while raising his eyebrow he said, "Yeah, What's up? What's on your mind?" Seeing the look he gave me, I attempted to reassure him that I wasn't about to ask him a stupid question, so I said, "It ain't no stupid question, I was just thinking about it, that's all." Curious to know what I was about to ask, he responded, "You good lil homie, just go ahead and say what you finna ask me."

Chewing down a delicious piece of conch I said, "Do you live by yourself?" Looking at me in confusion, he replied, "Yeah – why what's up?" That's when I followed with, "I don't know I was just thinking about it since you say you're going to be picking me up from school from now on. You think I can just live with you at your spot? That way it'll be easier for both of us."

Bam placed his styrofoam plate on the hood of the car and wiped his hands with a crumbled napkin.

Swallowing the last bit of food in his mouth, he looked at me and said, "Naw man, I wish you could, but you can't stay with me. My place ain't where it's at, I kind of like to have my own space though, you feel me? Besides what's wrong with living at your old girl crib? What she be tripping on you or something?" Feeling let down by his response, I solemnly shook my head in disappointment, as I looked down at my plate of food.

"Aye man, don't even sweat that shit lil homie," Bam said. "My old girl used to be tripping on me too, until I got tired of her shit, started making this paper and decided I was going to get up out of her crib for good. Don't even worry about it man, that's why I'ma look out for you cause I can already see it in your face that you be stressing all the time. I'ma teach you how to make this bread, so you ain't never got to be out here worrying about nobody but your damn self, you heard me."

Still not ready to go back home yet, I said, "Aye Bam, you got a game system at your crib?" He replied, "Yeah but we ain't bout to go to my spot though, I got some people over there cleaning up real quick," which was his code for him having people at his house counting money and bagging up drugs.

"But I'ma take you to my homie crib though, he got one. We can head over there later, so I can spank you in Madden or NBA 2K, real quick." I laughed at him and said, "Man you can't play Madden, you like forty years old." Shortly after that conversation, he tapped me on my knee as I sat on the hood of the car and told me to hop off the car so we could head out. We threw our food containers into a nearby trash can, jumped in his Mustang and headed out.

That day we spent the entire afternoon together. It was like a breath of fresh air for me, as I got to meet some of his homies from the north side of town. He felt comfortable enough to show me where he had a few of his lil trap spots located. Bam said to me as we rode in the car, "Aye lil homie, one day all of this could be yours if you play your cards right. You just got to work hard for it, you feel me.

"Out here in these streets don't nobody care about you, so you got to make sure you protect what's yours at all times. You can't be out here in these streets thinking that shit sweet cause somebody'll come right up to you and light your lil ass up without warning. See, I can teach you how to handle your own, but I ain't going to be out here babysitting your ass, you feel me.

"When you with me, you got to pick up on shit real fast cause every second we out here count. You got to make sure that your every move is well calculated so there ain't no room for error, cause if you slip up out here - boy yo ass might get killed. You hear me lil homie?" he said as we rode through the shadowy street of Liberty City.

"Yeah, I feel you," I said, as I imagined what life would be like once I got enough money to get my own spot, get my own car and finally be able to get the hell out of my mama house just like Bam did. We were a few blocks away from my house when Bam decided to ask me, "So, you think you ready to be down?" With my heart thumping because I knew that if I said, "Yes," there was no turning back and that if I said, "No," I'd probably be missing out on my chance to finally gain my independence from my mom. So, with a slow and elongated pause, I replied, "Yeah, I'm ready."

Bam looked over at me and said, "Now you know there ain't no switching up once you in lil homie. Once you in, you in for life and the only way you get out is if somebody take you out or if I take you out myself." Knowing how serious this was, I tried to look as calm and collective as possible so that Bam didn't suspect me of being soft, even though I knew I was about to get myself into something I couldn't get out of.

Pulling up in front my house, he turned the car off and scooted up in his seat to pull out his wallet from his back pocket. Glancing over, I could see him flipping back a wad of one-hundred-dollar bills. He then, took out three of them and handed them over to me saying, "Here, now you can do either one of two things with this money: Save this up so you can try to get up out of your old girls shit as soon as possible or go ahead and treat yourself to something nice."

Hesitant to take the money, he said to impatiently, "Man, you better take this shit out of my hand before I change my mind." That's when I quickly snatched the money and shoved it into my right pocket. Bam said, "Aye just so you know; tomorrow is when you gon' to get made, Aight?" For some odd reason, when he said that, I thought he was talking about getting a Tattoo. I suppose it was because as he was talking to me, I was looking at all the Tattoos he had on his arms and neck.

I spewed out in a surprised voice, "I got to get a tattoo tomorrow?" Bursting in laughter, Bam looked at me and said, "Man you a trip. Naw, getting made ain't about getting no tattoo, it means you got to do something to get initiated. So, tomorrow, I'ma need you to prove to me that you down for real. You going to go with me to hit this lick on some fools in Edison Projects because they owe me some money and they were out here telling people that they ain't paying me shit."

Finding out what 'made' meant, I slightly glanced away thinking to myself, "Well DJ, this is what you wanted, so this is what you going to have to do." Spotting my lil brothers' dad pulling up in the yard, Bam said, "Aye lil homie, go ahead and go before you get in trouble with your folks. But listen, tomorrow don't expect me to pick you up after school. I'ma be handling something, so at like seven thirty, I want you to meet me at the fast food restaurant on Sixty-second street."

Before getting out the car, Bam he showed me how to do the handshake and signs so that I could practice. Leaving the car, I felt energized because I was finally gaining more of Bams' respect and trust. Plus, I just knew this was about to be the start something new, which made me excited and nervous at the same time. I felt like I was becoming a new man, one who knew what he was after and was going to go get it by any means.

When I fell asleep that night, I ended up waking up during the middle of a bad dream. The dream was so intense that it damn near felt like it was happening for real. Earlier that night, I went to sleep thinking about how I would go about hitting this lick with Bam and what I was going to spend my money three hundred dollars on. But in the dream, everything was all different.

It took place at my grandma Dee house; she had asked me to get something out of her kitchen. So, as I walked down the dim hallway towards the kitchen, I had this strange feeling that something was watching me. When I got in the kitchen, I looked inside of the oven, and there was nothing in it. I poked my head inside of the fridge and realized that I forgot what I had come into the kitchen to look for. That's when I heard someone softly call out my name, prompting me to turn around and say, "Huh?"

However, when I turned around, there was no one there. So, I brushed it off, walked over to the sink and started washing the dishes when I heard the voice again. Once more, I stopped what I was doing, turned around and tried to see who was calling me, but still, no one was there. I thought "Okay, I must be tripping or it could be the TV." Closing my eyes and shaking my head, I slowly turned around but immediately heard my name get called once more.

Quickly and in an irritated tone, I yelled, "WHAT?" But when I turned around this final time, I saw the most disturbing thing I had ever seen in my life.

Looking on the wall next to the fridge, I saw the pale face of my dead cousin Jaleel, staring at me from inside of a clock as he called out to me. Almost instantaneously, my body shut down in complete terror as his deteriorating face put me into a state of shock. His voice was eerie and hollow, as the elongated sound of my name synchronized with each tick of the clock.

I began to yell for help, but somehow no one could hear me. I attempted to run towards the living room hoping that someone would help me, but as I ran down the hallway, it seemed as if I was moving in slow motion and the walls were slowly closing in on me. Terrified and feeling helpless, it felt as though I was being sucked into a wormhole of fear. That's when out of nowhere, I woke up gasping for air, and to the sound of my television as it turned on from its programmed timer. I was sweating, out of breath and terrified, as I sat there trying to figure what in the hell kind of dream was that.

As the day went on in school, something about me just didn't feel right anymore because the whole time I couldn't stop thinking about that dream. What made my day even worse, was that my mom and I got into an argument this morning about some dirty dishes that Gary left in the sink. She swore me up and down that they were mine, as I tried to explain to her that I didn't even eat at home last time.

I sat in each class wondering about my dream the entire time that I almost forgot about meeting with Bam later. I kept trying figure out, "Why is Jaleel coming to me in my dreams all the time?" Leaving school, my nerves were all over the place. I couldn't sit still because to me it felt like everybody knew what I had planned with Bam after school.

I was so paranoid that during lunch when one of my boys walked up behind me and tapped me on the shoulder. I completely flipped out on him as he looked at me in confusion, saying to me, "Hold on bruh, chill out man – shit ain't even that serious." I was tripping, and it felt like my sensitivity level was cranked up to the max.

When school ended, I didn't want to head straight home because I was too nervous I'd end up laying down and falling asleep. So, I walked to this lil community park near the fast food joint I was supposed to meet Bam. I sat down on the bench as my legs trembled like a washing machine on spin cycle. It was so hot outside that my body started to feel sticky and itchy.

In the distance, I noticed someone walking towards me with a red backpack on and looking sort of suspicious. But as the person got closer I realized that it was just my boy Chad. He came up to me and said, "What's up fool? What you doing over here on this side of Da City? You don't know nobody over here."

Remembering what Bam said to me about not telling people my business, I lied to Chad by saying, "Nothing man, I just left from getting some food. What you doing over here?" That's when he replied, "Shit man, you know me. I am everywhere, but nowhere all at the same time, I'm like government," he joked around.

"Yeah true, true," I said while rocking back and forth. Chad then said, "Bruh how come every time I see you; you always look like you up to something? I don't know, but you look real suspicious sitting out her by yourself in this park with little children playing around." Offended by his comment, I replied, "What you trying to say?" as I turned around, looking at him with a serious face.

Finding my reaction funny, he chuckled and said, "See, I always know how to get to you boy." I responded, "Well, that ain't funny. It's people out here in this world that are real life pedophiles and I ain't one of em." Not making eye contact with Chad, I panned around the park trying to remain aware of my surroundings because he was right, I was in the wrong hood and didn't know anybody around here.

"Yo, why you keep looking around? Who you looking for?" he said to me, curiously. I replied, "None of your business. Why you always got to be so nosey all the damn time? Shit, you my boy and all but damn man, sometimes you got to learn how to mind your own business." Feeling disrespected by what I said, Chad stood up from the bench and shouted, "Chump what you mean mind my own business? I thought I was supposed to be your boy. You act like I'm out her asking you questions to set you up or something. If I had something going on or to tell you, you already know I would've put you up on game a long time ago. You tripping fool."

Realizing that, indeed I did just say some messed up crap to Chad, I looked at him and attempted to apologize. "Yeah, man you right," I said, "That's my fault bruh. It's just; I got something to going on right now that I really can't about." Chad looked at me funny and said playfully, "Man forget your apology. Now come on man, what's going on with you bruh? You already know you can talk to me about whatever. Plus, I don't like the way you keep looking around out here like somebody about to come rob you or something, you making my nerves bad."

I turned my head, and stared at him silently, when he replied, "Man, are you going to tell me what the hell is up or what?" Reluctantly, I responed to him, "I'm supposed to be meeting up with my cousin Bam so that I can get 'made' today. We're supposed to be going to the projects over there and hitting a lick on some dudes that owe him money. Damn, you happy now? I told you now leave me alone."

Looking at me with his eyes wide as ever, Chad replied, "Bruh, like what were you thinking? Are you serious right now? Do you know you can go to jail if you get caught? Or even worse, if anything goes wrong and them Haitians over there find out it was y'all trying to rob them, they going to kill y'all ass and your whole family.

"Yo, as your boy – real talk! I can't let you do this man. We'll go talk to Bam and tell him you changed your mind; I'm sure he'll understand where you come from cause this ain't like you dawg." I replied, "Yeah all that you saying sound good but it ain't as easy as you think it is. Bam ain't going to want to hear that and if he finds out that I was talking to you, it ain't no telling how he going to react towards me."

"Well, okay then - Mr. 'I got it all figured out,' then tell me – what exactly are you going to do then? You think that by joining some stupid ass gang, it supposed to make your balls bigger or give you some more juice on the streets? You don't realize that everybody we ever knew that got caught up with this gang shit either dead or sitting they ass in somebody prison over some bullshit. Don't be stupid your whole life DJ, you smarter than this. Besides, you about to put yo life on the line for somebody, when you barely even know this man. Come on man; you know that shit doesn't make no sense."

Not trying to entertain what Chad was saying to me, although the shit he was mentioning was the truth. I replied sadistically, "It is what it is." That's when Chad snapped and shouted, "Man you are a real jackass. You about to take a chance at throwing your whole life away or worse, losing your life because you feel like you got to prove yourself to another man. Bruh, you got to be out yo rabbit ass mind if you think I'ma sit here and listen to this bullshit, you must be crazy. Bout to ruin your whole life over some stupid shit."

Chad was getting on my nerves with his preaching so, I responded to him by saying, "Listen to me Bruh, I already told you that I made up my mind, so stop talking all that nonsense trying to make me rethink my decision before you and start having problems out here for real. As a matter of fact, it's almost about that time for me to meet up with Bam, so I'll holla at you later."

Reaching my hand out to shake Chads' before I left, he just stood there gawking at me with the face of absolute disgust. So, I pulled my hand back, shrugged my shoulders and said, "Aight then Bruh, be easy," before heading to meet with Bam.

As I walked up to the parking lot of the fast food joint, I didn't see Bams' car. Suddenly, I saw a hand wave at me out of this black Toyota. It was Bam signaling me to hurry up, so I started jogging towards the car. When I got in, I felt kind of good using the handshake he taught me yesterday, as he said, "Damn lil homie I see you catch on quick." Grinning widely, "I said - yeah man. I told you, I'm trying to get like you one day."

Hearing me say that, must've made him feel warm on the inside as he replied, "Man, I swear you remind me of myself sometimes. Just young and dumb but full of potential." But quickly, the conversation went from all fun & games, to business. "Well, aight lil homie, you ready to handle this?" Bam said to me with a serious tone.

Nervous and filled with anxiousness I responded, "Yeah, let's do this." That's when Bam handed me some black gloves, a black ski mask, and a 9mm pistol before we backed out of the parking lot and began to head down the main street towards the projects. In the car, there was a moment of ominous silence that made my skin crawl, as I could feel my legs twitching from the nervousness.

We pulled up next to a few cars in a half empty parking lot close to where we were going to hit the lick. As Bam parked the car, he said, "The busters that owe me money are two blocks over, you hear the music playing?" I whispered, "Yeah, I hear it." He replied, "Good - cause that's them punks, and that's where we going."

After he had parked, Bam instructed me to put on my gloves and to wipe down the gun with the red bandana he just gave me. Then he said, "Alright - so, this the plan lil homie. What we're going to do is, we going to go separate ways." As soon this man mentioned splitting up, my heart began to pound so hard that chest my started hurting.

"Once we get out, I want you to take the long route around the block. Walk on the main street, this way when I sneak out from behind the building, you can pop out on the other side of the road and point the gun at them while I lay them down. But you got to keep an eye on everybody at all times so that you can make sure ain't nobody trying nothing slick, alright – you hear me?" Bam said.

"Yeah, I got you," I responded while visibly trying to stop my left leg from shaking. Bam reached out and grabbed me by my left shoulder. With the muffled sound of his voice from the ski mask blocking his mouth he said, "Aye listen to me, it's going to be alright lil homie. I know you scared because it's your first time. Shit, I was afraid the first time I hit a lick too but once you get out here and knock this first one out, all the rest of em' going to be like boiling water on a stove top. It's your time to shine, so we going to get in there and get out of there as smooth as possible."

Feeling a bit confident by Bams' pep talk, I was still worried, but now I was ready to go. Shortly after, he dapped me up, and we slowly crept out the car before taking off in our separate directions. Shook that I was going through with this, I headed towards the main street like a man on a mission.

I made sure that I was walking normal just like Bam said but I wasn't used to holding a gun in my pocket, so I kept pulling my pants up to prevent them from sagging because of how heavy the gun was. Walking pass the road that the dudes we were about to rob were on, to the left of me I could see that they were all drinking and smoking, as loud music played from this Brown Box Chevy.

I hurried across the street so that no one would look down the block and see me passing. As I made the quick left to head behind the houses that were on the opposite side of the street that the dudes were on. I heard someone one whispering my name. Completely on edge, I pulled out the gun and turned around, only to see that it was Chad.

I whispered in anger, "What in the hell are you doing here man, I could've shot you." He said, "I couldn't let it sit on my conscience that I allowed you to leave and didn't do all I could to stop you because God forbid something bad was to happen, I don't think I'd ever be able to come back from that." I responded, "Man, get yo ass out of here before you get us both killed" as I tried to push him away.

"No man, he said. You don't need to be doing this. Just think about what your mom would say if she knew you were out here about to rob people because you were trying to get into some petty ass gang." Upset that he even mentioned my mama, I replied, "I don't give a damn about what my mama thinks. She doesn't give a damn about what I do anyway. She doesn't even listen to anything I got to say anyway, so go on somewhere before I shoot yo ass."

"Bruh, I'm not going nowhere. I don't feel good about this anyway, and I know you don't either. Come on, let's get out of here before it's too late, we still got time," Chad said to me. Pausing in frustration, "I grabbed Chad by the collar of his shirt and said, "Look, Bruh - I'm not leaving. I ain't come all this way just to back out now, and if you don't agree with what I'm about to do, then that's on you."

I shoved him back and turned away to head behind the bushes, but this idiot kept following me, trying to convince me that I needed to leave. "Bruh, I'm begging you to just listen to me for once, this ain't you - I know this ain't you DJ. You are better than this man. You can still make it out of this." Yelling back in a low voice, while slightly tearing up, I responded, "I CAN'T.

"You don't understand, If I don't go out there, then he gon' die and if he don't die, then he going to kill me because I left him hanging. I ain't got no other choice, so just bounce man." In that same moment, all I could hear was the piercing sound of a lady screaming and then a voice yelling, "Get Down! Get Down the on goddamn the ground."

Adrenaline rushed through my body like the electric current of hot telephone wires. I ran with an urgency to get over there and help Bam, but in doing so, I mistakenly dropped my gun. Scrambling back to pick it up, I struggled to put on my ski mask as I made my way through the darkness of the night.

Finally, I ran out onto the street with my gun pointed out. Seeing my late entrance, Bam screamed at me, "Yo! What in the hell took you so long? Get your shit together. Ain't nobody got time to be waiting on you. I told you, let's get in and get out." Apprehensively I replied, "My bad, I dropped my gun."

"Dropped yo gun? Man back the hell up and make sure you watch these busters, while I check their pockets. Hold your damn gun with two hands, so you don't drop it," Bam yelled.

I stood there watching it all take place; it seemed

like the world had slowed down as my heart beat slowly began to synchronize with the seconds of time. I couldn't believe what I was doing, as I carefully watched Bam standing over the people and digging into each of their pockets in search of money.

Frustrated that he couldn't find anything, Bam started asking everybody, "Where the hell my money at?" But when one of the dudes moved a little bit too much, Bam kicked him dead in the face - knocking him out cold and sending blood splattering across the pavement.

"Anybody else got something to say other than to tell me where the hell my money at?" he said. Locked in on the guy that was just kicked in the face, I stood there motionless as my jaw fell to the asphalt. It felt like this whole moment was something straight out of a movie and at any time now the director was going to yell cut. Feeling sympathetic for the dude that just got kicked and the pregnant woman that was lying next to him crying, I yelled out, "Aye, Bam I think it's time to go. They ain't got nothing; we got to go."

Fiercely turning his head towards me, Bam yelled out, "What!? Did you just say my god damn?" before thunderously walking over and slapping the shit of me. He struck me up the side of my head so hard that my ear started ringing. "My bad, I ain't mean to say your name," I whimpered, as I curled my body bracing myself for another blow.

"My bad? There ain't no damn, 'My bad.' Now,

these idiots know who trying to rob them all because of yo stupid ass. So, thanks to you, now I got to kill everybody," he said to me, before snatching the gun out of my hand and slowly turning away towards the people pleading for the life on the ground. I swear the wickedness of his voice and the look of death in his eyes was unlike anything that I had ever seen before.

Walking back over to the sidewalk, where the people were laying. I paced frantically, with my hands on my head, as the deep feeling of regret circulated through my veins. I listened to the screams of a pregnant woman pleading for her life. As Bam stood over her pointing his gun, he didn't even get a chance to let one shot off, when all I heard was the sound of a loud "BOOM!" That woke the entire block up, as Bam body went jerking backwards. Trying to maintain his balance because he had been shot, Bam started to carelessly let off shots in every direction.

I quickly took cover behind a parked car, covering my throbbing ears, as I panned my eyes through the window of the car to see where the shot had come from. At a distance, and to the far right of where Bam was standing, there was a huge mist of smoke floating from the bushes. Then this heavy-set guy with long dreads, wearing a black T-shirt, slowly walked out of the darkness, wielding a twelve-cage shotgun and blasted off a second fatal shot that sent Bam hurling backward.

Without hesitation, I turned around and ran for my life as quickly as I could. The feeling was just like Gary said it would be. I was moving so fast, that I could feel the wind pressing against my face, as it whistled in my ears. The sound of guns shots and bullets colliding with the walls followed me, but it didn't matter because the only thing I had on my mind was to 'survive.'

I ran full speed until I made my way back way back to the fast food joint and hid behind their huge industrial trash can. I stayed there crouching down, with my heart beating through my chest, hoping that no one followed me before falling to my knees and bursting into tears. I couldn't believe it, I just almost died but most of all, Bam was dead. I laid there crying, when shortly after, Chad startled me as he frantically came searching for me.

"Yo DJ! DJ!" he said. "You Aight? I the heard guns shots man." But at that moment, I couldn't give him a response. The only thing I could do was sit there crying as my stomach begins to feel hollow and I started to feel sick.

Seeing how distraught I was, Chad sat next to as I cried and asked again, "Yo, DJ, you aight homie? Yo ain't shot or nothing, right? Where's Bam?" But as he asked that question, the tears began to pour even harder. He asked again but this time in a much softer tone, as if he was hoping that I didn't say the worst. Trying to hold back the flood of tears I replied, "He gone man, he gone," as I kicked my feet and pounded my fist on the concrete.

Sitting there in disbelief of what I just told him, Chad attempted to comfort me by saying, "Bruh, it's going to be alright," as tears slowly trickled from his eyes. "It's going to be alright, I promise." After a while, I just laid there speechless, thinking about how things could've gone differently if I had done what I was supposed to or if I never even agreed to go.

CHAPTER 7

RED VELVET

"SLIME, WHAT'S GOOD with you boy?" One of my homies said as he approached me in the school hallway. "Nothing, just vibing," I replied while reaching out to dap him up. "Boy you ain't never in class man, what you doing in the hallway?" he asked me. "Bout to head to the bathroom real quick to handle something," I told him. "Oh true, what you got to take a dump?" he said to me trying to be humorous. "Naw man," I responded looking at him with a serious face. Realizing I wasn't in a joking mood, he said to me, "Oh my bad man, you good - everything straight?" As he could sense that something was bothering me. Looking at him intensely, I replied, "Naw, you remember I told you how me and Devon made a bet on the football game between the Da West and Central?"

"Yeah, I remember y'all making that bet why wassup?" He replied to me with his ears now tuned into the conversation. "Well, this mud still ain't pay me my money yet for losing that bet and every time I ask him for my money he always talking about, 'I ain't got it.'

"Fool always trying to hit me with that bull saying, 'Oh, naw man. I'm broke, but I got you as soon as I get it.' I swear this dude going to learn to stop trying to buck me for my cash," I said angrily. "Dang, boy, I thought he would've paid you by now," my boy told me, still shocked that I hadn't been paid. "Matter of fact, what class buddy in? We can handle this right now. You tripping DJ, how you gon' let this mud go two whole months without paying you your cash? You trying to go handle this or what?" He asked me, seemingly just as fired up about the situation as I was.

"Bruh, he in the bathroom right now shooting dice with Cam them," I responded in a confirming voice. "Oh yeah, well shit - let's go get his ass right now then," my boy said excitedly. "Buddy going to learn about playing with your money dawg. On the real though, I don't know who he thinks we are but we A.B.M over here – Always Bout that Money, so if he thinks it's a game out here, then we going to show him what kind of games we play then."

Feeling even more pumped up now that my boy was about to roll with me, I dapped him up and said, "Aight then homie, lets ride," as we headed towards the boy's bathroom on the second floor of the three-story school building.

Making our way over he said, "Oh yeah, I forgot to ask you, but Aye - I think I might need to cop some more of that loud from you after school cause my bomb don' ran low and people been asking me when I'm going to re-up all day." Not really focused on what he was asking me for at that moment, I responded to him, "Yeah, yeah - I got you, but we'll talk about that later though, right now I'm just thinking about getting my paper out this soft ass jit you feel me?"

My homie nodded his head quickly while saying "You right, you right. Which bathroom they in?" I pointed to the one down the hall by the stairway on the east wing of the building. He squinted his eyes and said, "Bet! Let's speed up a lil bit before the security guards come and try to make us get back to class."

Putting a little pep in our step, he started laughing while saying, "Man this mud don't even know he bout to get flipped today if he ain't got your money. How he going to be gambling but saying he broke?" Sucked his teeth and blurted "Buddy tripping."

Not responding to him and just wishing that he would shut up because he was one of my more talkative homies. The one that made all the jokes and sometimes didn't know when to put the lid on his mouth. I was more reserved and didn't express my emotions that often but people knew who I was and they respected me because of that.

Trying to tune him out as we approached the bathroom door, I grabbed him by the shirt and pulled him back before we entered. I stood in front of him and whispered, "Aye look, when we go in there, we going to walk in and vibe at first, aight? I want him to think that everything straight. So I'ma hop in the crap game and get down with fifty. Cam told me that Devon been hot all day, throwing trips and rolling sixes, so when I pull my rag out of my pocket – you already know what time it is."

Rubbing his hands together, while licking his lips my homie said, "You already know me boy. This buster about to see what time it is." My homie was about five eleven and straight muscle. He was never really that involved in sports but for some reason and just like almost every other dude that lived in Da City, he was built strong and quick as hell.

He held the door open for me as we walked inside. There was Cam with his red and white Jordan sevens on, as usual, standing with about five other dudes that we knew from around the hood and being in school. Then, there was that buster Devon standing over there smiling at me. As soon I walked in, he was the first person to say, "What's up!" as he stood next to an open bathroom stall.

"DJ! Boy, what's up with you, you came to get down?" this Buster said to me. Nonchalantly, I replied, "Yeah - I came to get down." But, I had something else in mind, that had nothing to do with trying to win this crap game. One of the dudes in the bathroom was shaking the dice in his hand saying, "It's a dub or better," meaning that to place a bet in the dice game, I had to start my bet off at twenty dollars.

"Aight," I replied, but as we moved through the cramped bathroom dapping everybody, I made sure that I dapped this sucker Devon up last. Then I walked over to the other side of the dice game circle, closer to the sink near the door, standing directly on the opposite side of Devon so that I could watch his ass. My homie stood next to Devon and started joking around with him, trying to make everything seem just fine.

With all bets in, the dice game was ready to begin. A few dudes had taken turns before me, rolling three's and higher but when my turn came around. I shot out a deuce, which meant I was now on the losing end of the game. As the dice found its way around the circle, they finally reached the hands of Devon.

He was pissing me off because he had already owed me money, but now he was being boastful by widening his arms and telling people to move back, while spreading his legs widely before he rolled. Shaking up the dice, he pointed at me and said, "This one for you DJ," as he blew on the dice, shook them up some more and slung them to the ground, while snapping his fingers together and repeating the phrase, "Head Crack!" after each unsuccessful roll.

Rolling out nothing playable, he picked the dice up

one last time before saying, "Dang - DJ boy, you must be bad luck. I ain't been rolling nothing but sixes all day until you got in here. Here, blow on the dice for me, he said to this dude standing next to him in a playfully taunting manner. "Hopefully, it blows away DJ's bad luck he done brought in here."

Feeling confident that he was going to win, he uttered, "Third times a charm, I can feel it in my arm," as he threw the dice once more, hoping for a winning roll. Looking at the green and red dice roll against that tile floor, I was hoping that he'd lose. But as the dice came to a slow halt, once again this fool Devon won. The dice landed with two of them on the number four and one dice with the number six.

He shouted, "What I told y'all - Pay up!" As he taunted everyone. The dude in charge of collecting the money from underneath everyone's shoe swept across the board. When he attempted to pull the dub from underneath my foot, I applied pressure to it and said to him, "Watch out, Yo!" Looking up at me confused, he replied, "Come on man, you got to pay up. You loss. If you don't pay, the house don't get paid bruh."

With a little more strain in my voice, I looked directly into his eyes, reinforcing my words by saying, "I said Watch out, yo!" Throwing his hands up in surrender, he shook his head and scooted over to the next person as he understood that I wasn't about to give up my money. Almost without hesitation, Devon blurted, "DJ come on man you loss, pay up bruh."

Turning my head sideways to mean mug him, I replied, "What! Who you think you talking to buster?" As the anger boiling inside of me was moments away from spewing out. My thoughts became narrower, the claustrophobic energy of the room intensified, and the dim lights appeared to get dimmer along with the foul smell of unflushed piss becoming fainter.

"Pay up!" He said in a demanding tone. I'm guessing; he thought that by saying it a second time it made him look courageous. "Buster, I don't know who you think you talking to but you ain't about to get shit from me," I responded. One of the dudes in the bathroom inserted, "Come on man, you wilding DJ. It ain't even that serious." So, I turned towards him and gave him a look that suggested; he should probably mind his own business.

Devon responded, "Man you on some other shit boy I tell you. I ain't got time to be playing these games with you dawg. You always think you run or own some shit. Man, y'all just run it back. I'ma just let it slide. Fool be tripping," he said, while looking over at my homie Cam.

Hyped by what he was saying, I blurted out, "If yo soft ass got something to say, then why don't you say that shit to my face you lying ass duck." Upset by my disrespectful comment, he looked over at me and said, "Duck? Who you calling a Duck? Man, you tripping for real DJ - I ain't on all that rah-rah you over there talking," while cracking his knuckles with a few bills in his hands.

Slightly leaning back, placing my hands in front of my crotch, I replied cynically, "Oh so you think it's a game, huh?" For me, having him talk to me like this in front of all these dudes was completely unacceptable. Laughing, I said, "You know you really funny boy. I just don't understand, how you out here gambling but somehow never have money to pay me back. I just think that's real funny fool."

Pissed off, he said, "Bruh, I told you I was going to give you that two fifty when I got it but now you ain't getting shit, and that's on my mama. You ain't going to come up in here and try to put down on me like I'm one of these other dudes you be running that shit on. You got me messed up. You either going to take it out my pocket or shoot me a clean 1-on-1 fade."

I could see that my boy standing directly next to him was livid, as he looked at me with his eyes cocked wide open, hoping that at any moment I'll give him the signal. But seeing that I must've been taking too long for him, without warning my homie turned sideways, cocked his arm back and with all the force he had in his body, punched the shit out Devon.

A loud 'CLACK' sounded off, as he sent Devon flying through the halfway open door of a bathroom stall. Pushing my way through the other guys standing around, I ran over and began to stomp on Devon's curled up body, as he attempted to shield his head from the bottom of my shoe.

By now, everybody in the bathroom panicked and ran out, while we remained to show Devon we meant business. Cam was a big sneaker head, so as we stumped dude out, Cam was snatching off his shoes.

It was like my mind had drawn a blank and went somewhere else as my foot repeatedly crashed down on his helpless body. Everyone's voice sounded muffled to me, images of Bam flashed before me, and my foot appeared to be stuck in autopilot. I couldn't even feel Cam tapping on my shoulder, trying to get me to stop by telling me, "Yo, Let's Go."

I was infuriated, and it seemed like all the anger I had built inside of me because of everything else in my life, just unleashed all at once. Stomping him, I could see his terrified soul whimper as he pleaded for me to stop. It took both of my homies to pull me away, but as I remained trapped in this moment of rage, I picked up a trash can and threw it over the stall at him. Shouting, "Don't ever play with my money, you green ass buster," as we dashed out of the bathroom.

After jumping Devon, we all ran back to class and attempted to act calm as if nothing ever happened. When I arrived to class thirty minutes later than I was supposed to, my teacher was pissed as she threatened to write me a referral for skipping.

Sitting in class, it felt as though my time was running out and at any moment I'd see the police along with the school principal busting through the door to arrest me. Not being able to sit still, I kept switching positions in my chair, while nervously tapping on the desk with my pen. My legs were shaking so vigorously, that it made the desk vibrate.

Out of all the crazy things I've done, this was most definitely on the list of the dumbest things ever. I just knew that Devon was downstairs snitching on us and never having been to jail before, the thought of it made my stomach cringe with regret.

I could've just waited until after school; I tried to convince myself. The image of sitting in a prison cell and not being able to see my friends or family was unsettling. Plus, I heard that the Dade County jail was an overcrowded death trapped, infested with pest and dudes awaiting a trial that did whatever they wanted because they felt as though they had nothing to lose.

The clock was ticking slowly as the teacher continued to go on about how we're going to be seniors next year and the changes we needed to make in life, but in almost perfect timing the bell rang, cutting her sermon short. Paranoid and on high alert I thought to myself, "Shit, they must be waiting for us downstairs." So, to avoid being arrested, I maneuvered through the back exits of the school just in case they were looking for me.

Speed walking through the bolstering hot Miami sun and cutting through oncoming traffic, I safely reached home. Heading straight to my room, I kicked off my shoes and collapsed on top of my bed, as the feeling of relief saturated my soul. Laying there motionless, I couldn't help but think to myself, "What am I doing? Things are getting way out of control."

Taking a short nap, I rose from my deep sleep and prepared to take a shower. Allowing the soothing hot water to rinse over my body, I showered in the darkness, letting my mind wander into another realm of consciousness. It gave me the opportunity to reflect on my life and all the things that I had been experiencing.

Amidst the darkness of the room, I saw all the faces of those that I had loved and lost to the harsh realities of the world. Some whose soul was as pure as honey and others who were unpleasant products of the sick world we occupied. Their faces manifested to me with the expressions of hopefulness and regret.

My soul would grow weary, as I slumped down and questioned my existence in this world. "Why was I still here? How come everyone around me was dying by either senseless gun violence, being locked up for the rest of their life or just completely disappearing out of my life?" I asked myself."

Loneliness swallowed the dark pits of my heart, causing my soul to ache for the appreciation and understanding of others. I was only doing the best that I could do with the cards that I was given, but somehow the efforts I made to do good by others never seemed to be acknowledged. My world was barred between the feelings disappointment and doubt, as I struggled to hold myself together during some of the roughest days when I just wanted to give up on life.

Staring in the mirror at a reflection that appeared foreign, I looked upon him in search of clarity, as the skin we both wore could never synchronize our thoughts. I was becoming a desperate soul, imprisoned by a life of longing to find internal peace. Life was all but a dream, and the reality of it was that I didn't have a damn clue as to what my purpose was in life. That is - until I met her.

As my junior year of high school came to an end, I was surprised that I had even lived long enough to see it happen. One Saturday, when I was at this family BBQ with my mama and little brother, my soulmate and I would have our first encounter. Kids were running around; adults were drinking as the laughter of conversations about the last time they had seen each other filled the vibrant atmosphere.

Heading to grab some food, I found myself making a quick double take when I saw this lovely caramel complexion sister wearing a yellow and white shoulder strapped floral dress. Her long brown hair reached just below her shoulder blades, as it gracefully flowed with the rhythm of the wind, while she playfully chased a little kid in an open patch of grass.

Staring hard because she seized my attention, with my elbow I nudged my cousin standing in front of me fixing a plate of food and curiously asked, "Aye yo fam, who that over there?" Turning around slowly, while licking his fingers clean of the dripping baked bean juice, he replied to me, "Who you talking bout cuzo?" With the tip of my fork and trying not to look creepy, I pointed over at her saying, "Shawty right there! The one with the yellow dress on."

He replied, "Oh, her?" Irritably I quickly responded, "Yes man! Dang, who is she?" My cousin then said in a meddlesome manner. "Oh, that's Sierra bruh, why wassup? You trying to holla at her?" Lying to him, I responded, "Naw man. I'm just asking to ask but she some kin to us though?" He looked at me like, "Dude you going to sit up here and lie to me like this." Then I glanced at him and replied, "What? What you looking at me like that for?"

Smirking, he laughed and said, "Cause yo ass lying that's why. But naw she ain't no kin to us. I'm surprised you never saw her before, she go to Da West though." Shocked by this discovery, I immediately said, "Naw you lying bruh, she don't go out there. I know damn near everybody out there and I ain't never seen her out there." He then replied to me, "Man how you going to tell me? You don't even know her fool."

"I'm just saying, I ain't never see her out there. That's crazy," I responded. "But I'm saying though, since she not any kin to us, who she knows in our family? Who she came out here with?" In a shady remark, he said to me, "If you were around more often, then maybe you'd know who she was, but that's a different story. Anyway, that's Jayla best friend, they both grew up together." Happy to know that she was friends with my favorite lil cousin Jayla, I smiled and said, "Oh, Aight then, I'ma have to go holla at Jayla real quick."

"I thought you weren't trying to holla, you ole lying ass lil buster," my cousin, said to me as he laughed. I returned by saying, "Aye, you just make sure your fat ass don't eat up all the ribs and macaroni," teasing him about his weight. The whole time we were there, I couldn't stop staring at her as she walked around the park. I kept thinking to myself, "How come I had never seen her around the school yard?" It wasn't long before I built up the courage to call my cousin Jayla over and ask about her friend.

I yelled out, "Aye Jayla! Check me out real quick," as I stood so far away that I was nearly standing in the parking lot of the park. I attempted to remain discrete about my intentions as she approached me. "Hey DJ, what's up cousin?" she said while reaching in to give me a hug.

"Nothing much Jay, what you been up to?" I asked her. "I've been good DJ. Just school stuff and going to church. How about yourself?" she asked. With so much going on in my life, I thought about giving her the real answer to that question, but instead, I replied, "You know, the same ole, same ole. Just doing what I got to do, to get this money you feel me?"

She looked at me with her hand on her hip and said, "Boy, when are you going to stop all of that nonsense? You know the Lord is always here to redeem you, you just have to repent and ask him for his forgiveness." Zoning out as she went on with her church stuff, I replied, "Yeah, I feel you, Jay. I'm trying to get myself straight, I'ma start coming to church one of these days. That's kind of why I called you over here."

Looking at me in disbelief, she replied, "So what you about to start coming to church with us on Sundays?" I looked at her and said, "Yeah, if I'm free. Don't forget I used to go with y'all all the time when we were jits. It's just I had a lot going on but now that I'm getting myself situated I'ma be coming for real."

Still unconvinced Jayla said, "Okay DJ if you say so. Well, I'm glad you're getting it together, but I'm about to go back over there with my friend. I don't want her to feel left out." That's when I responded, "Aye, hold on, hold on Jayla. Who your friend is though?" She turned around to look at Sierra before saying in a defensive voice, "You talking about Sierra? Nun, Uhn. What you want with her?"

Grabbing her gently by the arm, and pulling her closer to me, I whispered, "Dang man, you ain't got to be so loud yo." But she snatched her arm out of my grip and stepped back, she responded with, "Boy ain't nobody being loud. How is she going to hear us way over here?" Insecure and shy about this conversation, my whole mood changed once I started to ask about Sierra. I replied, "Just chill Jayla, but listen, like on the real though. Do she talk to somebody?"

Jayla looked me up and down before saying, "You

think she going to want to speak to you? Ha - boy get a life?" as she began to laugh. Feeling offended, I asked, "What you mean? You know me, Jayla, you know I ain't no bad dude. When I get a girl, I treat her with respect. Plus, I make sure I buy her anything she wants." Continuing to laugh at me she replied, "Boy, that girl don't want your little bit of money, and I highly doubt that you're her type anyway. You barely go to school, and she doesn't like fake thug looking, dudes, no way."

"Man, ain't nobody faking like I'm a thug, you already know what time it is Jayla but that ain't got nothing to do with what I just asked you. Is she single?" I said as the unsettling feeling of rejection slowly crept upon my soul. "Boy, I don't know. Why don't you go ask her yourself?" she said before turning around and walking away.

As Jayla went back over to sit down with Sierra, I could see that she was now pointing at me, while Sierra began to squint her eyes over in my direction. I quickly turned around, embarrassed that she might've gone over there talking bad about me to Sierra. I just knew that there was no way I was going to be able to get this girl now.

Thinking of a way out, I leaped across and small wooden fence, taking the long way around the park, trying to get back over to mom and little brother. For some reason, I was always reluctant when it came to approaching girls. I always knew what to say because of the long talks I would have with Big Mike before he passed away from a heart attack a few years ago. I just didn't know how to get the words to come out as I wanted them.

Getting back to school the following week, I felt rejuvenated because something about wanting to hook up with Sierra just motivated me to do better. Even the conversation with my cousin Jayla caused me to feel like I had a chip on my shoulder, making me want to prove her wrong. Walking in the hallways to class or just sitting in the courtyard for lunch, I noticed Sierra as she talked with her friends but I never got the courage to walk over and say something. It wasn't until one day that she came to escort me out of class because I had been called down for an indoor suspension due to skipping class a while back.

Escorting me through the windy hallway, we were left with this awkward silence as our footsteps echoed throughout the hall. My heart beat increased, my body started to feel steamy, and my head began to feel itchy as my nervousness kicked in. Then finally, I broke the silence by saying, "So, your name Sierra, right?"

Without even looking at me she responded with a straightforward and nonchalant, "Yeah." Hearing that, I thought to myself, "Damn, what else should I ask her?" as my tongue began to feel heavy as a brick. Cautiously, I then said, "Ain't you friends with my cousin Jayla? Like y'all supposed to be best friends or something, right?"

Slightly rolling her eyes, while grinning she said sarcastically, "Yes, my name is Sierra, and I am Jayla's best friend, and yes, we saw each other at your family's picnic, any other obvious questions you want to ask me that you can answer yourself?"

Stunned by her sheer disregard for my feelings and how she just tried to shut me down. I gazed upon her, feeling impressed and slightly turned on by her fierceness. Jokingly I responded, "Well dang, you ain't have to shut me up like that, I was just trying to see if you were the same person because I don't see you around school that much." Cutting her eyes at me, she replied, "Boy stop lying. We see each other all the time; you just don't ever say anything to me when you see me."

"Oh snap, she be watching me," I said to myself. I responded, "Oh so you saw me this whole time, and you ain't say anything either? That's messed up." With a serious face, Sierra stopped walking and said, "I don't speak to nobody that don't talk to me." By the look she gave me, I could tell that it was one of those, "I been waiting for you," kind of looks. It made me feel stupid because this whole time I had been freaking myself out, thinking about all the things that could go wrong if I approached her.

Trying to sound smooth, I said to Sierra, "Well my bad, I ain't know you were cool like that, so I ain't never say anything to you, but now that I am aware I'll speak when I see you." She replied, "Uhm hmm, if you say so." Having this conversation with her made me feel kind of good on the inside, I felt as if I was making progress with her. But I knew that this conversation didn't mean anything. I had to keep my head on a swivel because if I slipped up and said anything wrong, this could all be a wrap.

As the gust of the wind from the air-conditioned double doors passed through the hallway, I caught a nice whiff of this edible flowery smelling perfume that she was wearing. I couldn't help but think about how much she sparked my interest and how I wanted to know more about her. It was also something about a woman that smelled good, that just put me into a trance-like state of mind.

Her essence was mysteriously captivating, and her voice was pleasant to the ears. Her mind was sharp as ever and conditioned to be something more magnificent than I could've ever imagined. Continuing down the hallway, we somehow began talking about who's going to buy lunch tomorrow.

I wasn't quite sure if she was feeling me just yet, but I was certain that I did make some good impression on her. Sierra's gorgeous brown and perfectly round eyes put my soul into an unknown realm of harmony. I didn't want to express my pure intentions at the time because I felt as though it was way too soon. Joking around as we stood outside of the room for indoor suspension, I looked at her and said, "So now that we're cool, can I get a hug?"

Smiling, she sarcastically replied, "I guess" before reaching in and giving me one of those sideways church hugs. Getting close to her, I became captivated with the scent of her irresistibly fresh smelling hair and the perfume she wore that was fit for a goddess like her, as she gave me that bubbly feeling of butterflies. Happy that we had finally gotten the chance to speak to one another, I remained doubtful of my progress, hoping that she didn't think I was doing too much to befriend her.

For the remainder of the school year, I would bring her lunch and began to sit with her, taking my time to get to know her, as well as, her friends. That's until she decided she'd like it better if we both just ate lunch somewhere else by ourselves so that we'd be able to spend time alone. My boys began mocking me as they grew more and more disappointed that I'd cancel on them too often because I was chilling with Sierra.

Together we'd have conversations about almost everything. From the people passing by us during lunch to her helping me out with some of my English and Math homework. The bond we were creating was maturing each day, and the feelings of deep emotion I gained for her followed suit.

She was a magical person, as it often felt as though we were on an island without any worries or stress. We'd became personal diaries for one another, as I expressed my deepest thoughts to her and she did the same to me. A lot of things that I told her were things that I had never even talked to my mom about such as me being there when Bam was killed.

But being the supportive and profoundly spiritual person that she was, Sierra would often talk to me about having faith because things happen for a reason. The two of us had been kicking it all summer, and when we weren't chilling together, we'd be on the phone talking all night until one of us ended up falling asleep.

Although everything seemed to be going just right and even better than I hoped for, I was still a little unsure if she felt the same way about me as I did for her because neither one of us ever brought that conversation up.

As summer came to an end, Sierra pleaded with me countlessly to come over to her house and meet her parents. The reason I fought this battle for so long was that I just felt like once they saw me, they'd judge me and question why Sierra even considered me as her friend. I wasn't one of the prep school, collared shirt and khaki pants wearing kind of dudes. I was straight from the hood, so I preferred to wear baggy jeans and tennis shoes.

Insisting that I stopped overreacting, Sierra finally convinced me to come through for a visit. As I got off the bus to head to her house, my heart was racing because I didn't know what to expect once I got there. Walking up to the address she had given me; I was stunned because her home was beautiful. On the outside, there was a large stone water fountain in the front yard, a huge two-car garage, and a U-shaped roundabout driveway.

Nervously, I rang the doorbell and in a few seconds, to the left of me I could see Sierra as she peeped her head through a white window curtain. Opening the door, the smell of chicken broth, sweet potatoes, and collards greens saturated the air. She said, "Hey DJ! I thought you weren't coming because I called your house and they said that they hadn't seen you since this morning." I responded, "Oh, so you don't have no faith in me huh? You thought I was just going to leave you hanging, right?"

Closing the door behind us, I walked into the house as she replied, "Boy please, don't act like you haven't stood me up before," while coming towards me for a hug. Looking at her, I had to adjust something behind my belt because DAMN was she looking good. She was wearing this tight fitted black dress that magnified all her developing features, causing me to briefly lose focus on why even came over. That's when she kindly asked me to leave my shoes by the door front because they had white carpet flooring and her mom would kill me if I walked over it with my shoes.

Looking around as we passed the living room area, I was in 'Awe' of the gold trimmed furniture and cream sofas they had covered with plastic. I even saw a bunch of trophies and autographed pictures placed on a shelf as we slowly walked towards the kitchen. Approaching their granite island counter top, I could see her mom cutting up chicken, as her dad sat on the far left in the living room watching a sports channel.

"Mom, DJs here," she said, alerting her mom to turn around and to my surprise she said jokingly, "Oh so this is the famous DJ that has my daughter up all night on the phone and spending all of our money at the mall?" as she rinsed her hands clean of chicken residue before coming over to greet me. Sierra's dad was so tuned into the television; he didn't even realize I was there until her mom yelled out, "John! Sierra's friend is here." Leading him to sluggishly rise from his seat and walk over to the kitchen to greet me. Standing in the kitchen, I felt intimidated with her dad towering over us, while her mom couldn't stop staring at me with the look of curiosity in her eyes.

Her dad said, "Oh so you're the guy my daughters' dating?" Swiftly, I turned my head to look at Sierra, as she denied it by saying, "No, No – we're just friends." Causing her mom to say, "Uhm hmm, that's exactly what John and I used to say until we ended up married." Laughing it off, her mom instructed Sierra to offer me something to drink and then asked if I was hungry because she was almost done cooking dinner.

Being over there, I instantly felt like I was at home. It was so cozy as they showed me respect from the moment I walked in, and it appears I had known them my entire life. Her dad and I joked in the living room, as he told me stories about his glory days of playing college basketball.

Following dinner, her parents decided that they were going to head into their room to give us a little privacy to hang out. Sierra then teased me by asking, "So you still scared?" I replied sarcastically, "Yeah- I'm scared. Scared of your breath that is," causing her to hit me in the head with one of the pillows on the couch.

As the sun was beginning to set, Sierra said to me, "Come on DJ, let's go outside into the back yard." Looking over to the right of me outside of a glass sliding door, I replied, "You trying to get me bit up by mosquitos?" She responded, "You such a pretty boy, I'm going to start calling you 'The Sweetness.'" I replied, "What!? I bet you won't say that again?" as I secretly grabbed hold of the pillow resting behind me. So, as she fixed her lips to repeat herself, I whacked her in the head with the pillow.

Getting hit, she quickly rose from her seat and charged me, playfully attempting to smack me in the face. We tussled for a few moments, before I managed to hold her arms down as she tried to bite my hands and arms. Laughing at her because she couldn't move, I asked, "Okay now, If I let you go, you going to leave alone so we can go outside?" But in an unconvincing voice, she said to me, "Sure."

Slowly releasing my grip, I pushed her away and jumped off the sofa so that she wouldn't retaliate, but as promised, she didn't come after me again. All she said was, "Don't worry. I'll get you next time." Sierra, then fixed her dress as she stood in the living room and headed towards the sliding doors to go outside.

Following behind her, I remained vigilant in case she attempted to try something sneaky. Outside, the sky resembled cotton candy, and the aroma of freshly cut grass filled the atmosphere. She strolled over to the trampoline in the back yard and began to jump on it. Initially, I stood at a distance just watching her gorgeous smile and luminous eyes as she stared back at me.

"Get on," she said. Hurrying over, I climbed onto the trampoline as well, and bounced around with her - as we challenged one another to a flip contest and tried to see who could jump the highest. But after a while, we eventually grew tired and started to lay down on the trampoline, just staring up at the stars.

I asked her, "How come your parents are so friendly?" She responded, "I don't know. That's just the way they are." I then said, "I mean, they let me come over, they fed me and even took the time out to talk to me. I just don't see how they are not tripping about you having a dude over at the crib, because I know if you were my daughter – shit - it wouldn't be none of that happening."

Sierra replied, "Well, that's why I'm not your daughter, and I don't know. I guess it's because they trust me enough to let me do certain things." Feeling a little insecure and fishing for information, I muttered, "or it could be that you always have dudes over here, so it's just normal for them?"

Mushing me in the face with the palm of her hand, she said, "Don't play with me. The only guy that has ever been over here was this dude named Jacob who they tried to hook me up with from the church and trust me - he got nowhere near as close to me as you have."

Smiling widely, I gazed up at the night sky. Then I paused before saying, "I guess that means I'm special then," as I turned my head to the left to see her reaction to my statement. Staring back into my eyes, she said softly, "I guess you are." I quickly turned my head back up towards the stars as a warm feeling took over my body. That's when she playfully pushed me and said, "But you ain't that special." I knew she only did that because she must've felt the energy surging through the atmosphere as things were starting to get a little warmer between us.

Moving to the other side of the trampoline to distance herself, Sierra replied, "How is your little girlfriend doing? Did you tell her you were coming over here? I don't want you to get in trouble if she finds out." Swiping at her feet with my hand, I responded, "Get in trouble by who? She don't run nothing over here, and I told you before if she got a problem with us chilling then she just going to have to deal with it, you're my best friend."

"Sure, DJ," she said to me in unpleased tone. I slowly crept back over to her and laid my head on her open arm. Rubbing my head, she said, "Well anyway, have you figured out what you're going to do about what you told me? Are you going to go see someone? Gazing at the moon, I responded, "Naw, I'll be straight." She replied, "I'm just saying DJ. Sometimes it's best you take care of that before it gets worse," but in response to her statement, I gently nudged her on the chin and said, "I think I'll be straight, that's what I got you for."

But to change the subject, I began to talk about her parents again. I said, "You know what I just realized?" Sierra responded, "What?" I replied, "I just realized that you don't look like either of your parents." Moving my head off her shoulder, she turned on her side and faced her back towards me.

Puzzled by her sudden movement, I leaned over and said, "Aye, what you moved my head for? I was just getting comfortable," but she didn't respond to me. Attempting to play around I started pushing down on the trampoline, forcing her to slightly bounce before she demanded me to "STOP!" Looking over her shoulder, I could see that she had begun to cry.

I quickly stopped and said, "Sierra, what's wrong?"

"Nothing," she replied, but I knew that she was lying. So, I moved her hair away from her face and told her to talk to me. That's when she sadly replied, "You wouldn't understand." Assertively I responded, "Understand what? What happened? Just tell me." I had to know what was bothering her because I'd never seen her cry before and I didn't like this.

She gradually scooted over, turned her body around to face me, while staring down at the trampoline in silence. Her eyes were glossy and flooded with tears. I pleaded again, "Sierra, please just tell me what's bothering you. I don't like seeing you like this." Closing her eyes, she slowly began to explain the reason by saying to me, "The reason I don't look like them because I'm adopted."

Struck by her confession, I could hardly come up with anything to say, so I replied, "Huh?" Continuing to whisper, she said, "When I was little, probably about six or seven years old. I used to get molested by one of my uncles. He would always tell me that I was his favorite niece and that I was going to grow up to be his wife when I got older.

I didn't know any better, but when he touched me, I just felt dirty. Sometimes he'd unzip his pants to rub his stuff on my face and then ask me to give it a wet kiss.

"I knew it was wrong, but I was so afraid to tell somebody because I didn't want people to think that I was lying or get him in trouble and he have him take his anger out on me again. My mama would've never believed me no way because she was always high on drugs and would hit me with almost anything. Since I was a lot darker than everybody else, she used to make fun of me by saying, I wasn't her child because all her babies were light skinned. I used to cry myself to sleep sometimes, hating myself for having darker skin than everyone else and just feeling like I was unwanted with nowhere else to go.

"It took for my uncle to come over to our house drunk one day for somebody to finally ask me, why was I so shy? I remember it like it was yesterday when he came stumbling into the apartment as my mom stood downstairs drinking beer and getting high with her friends. He walked up to me and said, 'Hey there cookie pudding. It's your favorite uncle Tony,' as he ran his wet beer smelling fingers across my face.

"I leaned my head away to avoid his dirty hands from touching me, but as usual he said, 'Look what uncle Tony got for you, I got you something,' as he fumbled through his pockets, dropping loose change onto the floor. 'Here, look what I got you baby girl. I got ten dollars for you today,' as he reached his hand out to give it to me.

"I just stood there nervously because I didn't want to take this money since I knew it only meant he was going to try to make me do something that I didn't want to do. That's when he raised his voice and yelled, 'Take the goddamn money, goddammit," causing me to jump backward in fear, before quickly snatching the ten dollars out of his hand.

"His eyes were hanging low like a bloodhound. His flimsy body swayed back and forth as he attempted to grab hold of his drunken balance. Placing his hand on the wall, he said to me, 'Ha, now that's what I'm talking about baby girl. You know you uncle Tony's favorite niece, right?'

"My brother and sister were only babies, so they didn't understand what was going on. He then stumbled back over to me, squatted down in front of me and whispered, 'Now, now why you don't say, 'Thank You,' and give uncle Tony some sugar, baby.' As he stood in front of me, I could feel the heat of his foul liquor smelling breath hitting my face, while he gave me this unforgettable perverted grin. 'Come on now,' he said, as he turned his head sideways, waiting for me to give him a kiss on his nappy beard. But as I unenthusiastically leaned in to kiss him, he forcefully grabbed my head and stuck his tongue down my throat.

"Stunned by his brazen move, I pushed myself away, as I vigorously wiped my tongue on the shoulder of my shirt to get that nasty taste of his thick, slimy, beer tasting saliva out of my mouth. Stumbling backward, he laughed before saying, 'Come on now baby girl, why you acting like that? You know uncle Tony was just playing with you. You ain't got to be running away from me.' Terrified, I could feel my heart quiver as I pleaded in my head for someone to come up here and save me. Staring deeply into my soul, he got up, turned around and locked the door, then slowly walked over and placed his beer on top of this broken TV we hand sitting in the living room.

"Calling out to me in a spine-chilling voice he said, 'Sierra! Come here, baby girl? I got something I want to show you.' But as I tried to hide behind the pillows placed on the sofa, I began to cry as I shook my head 'NO' in fear. I cried, 'No uncle Tony, please.' Demanding that I got up that instant, he yelled out to me, 'Now listen goddammit, I don't got time to be fooling around with your ass today. You sit up here and take my money, but now you act like you can't give me anything in return. I'ma tell your lil skinny ass one more time. Get your ass over here now, goddammit. Don't make me tell your ass to get over her again.'

"But still, I refused to get up. Hearing the voice of a woman outside of the window, I felt relieved because I thought it was my mom, but to my disappointment, the voice faded away down the hall along with my sense of hope that someone was going to save me. 'I'm going to count to three, goddammit and you better have your lil black ass over here before I'm done, or we're gon' have a goddamn problem, you hear me,' he yelled.

"I was so scared that my mind wouldn't allow my body to move and by the time he finished his countdown, I was still sitting on the sofa. That's when he charged towards me, picked me up by my skinny arms and squeezed me close to his musky body as I squirmed around crying. 'Didn't I tell yo little ass to get up?' he said to me.

"Whimpering as I looked over at my two and three-year siblings, I could only cry out for 'Help' as they stood there unaware of what was going on. Unpleased with my cries for help, he mumbled, 'Oh, so you want to cry today. Well, alright then, I'ma give ya lil ass something to cry about, as he quickly unfastened his belt, turned me around - shoving my head into the couch, while squeezing on my neck so hard that I could barely breathe.

"The next day when I went to school, I cried the entire time, as I could barely sit down in my chair. The bruises on my neck from his tight grip were so visible that my teacher noticed and sent me straight to the clinic. When I got there, they initially asked me, 'What happened?' and I told them, 'Nothing.' That was until this nice and funny social worker came in to talk to me.

"Her voice was so soothing, and after a long conversation, she finally convinced me to tell the truth. This lead to my uncle Tony being arrested for aggravated sexual assault of a child, causing my siblings and me to be taken away from mom by the state government, due to, child negligence. The three of us had to bounce around through foster homes for almost a year until that social worker lady showed up one day and adopted us all. So, that's the reason why I don't look like my mom and dad."

Listening to Sierra, my soul immediately went numb as I sat there visibly taken away by what she had just told me. At a loss for words, I couldn't figure out anything to say that would stop her from crying, so I just laid down next to her, pulled her in closer to me and placed her head on my chest, as I began to gently stroke my hand through her hair.

Speechless, I couldn't help but wonder about all the crazy things that I've been through and what would have my life been like if I never met her. Who knew that someone as beautiful and caring as she was, would have ever gone through something this heartbreaking? The level of appreciation I had for her, instantly grew to a new level as our souls began to merge.

As we laid there listening to the whistle of wind rustling against trees, crickets chirping a majestic tune of optimism and having her head planted against my chest, she softly called my name, "DJ!" I replied, "What's up?" That's when she asked me a question that I had never been asked before. She said to me, "Do you care if you live or die?"

Looking up, towards the light of the stars shining in the beautiful night sky, I took a deep breath and paused for a moment. I had to think about all the stupid shit that I'd been going through. I thought about the things I was doing with my life currently and what I planned to do in the future. At times, I felt as though my life was full of regret and with every day that passed, I hoped that somehow everything that I went through, would all make sense in the end. But with uncertainty, I softly replied to Sierra, "I mean, to be honest. I really don't know."

CHAPTER 8

NO UMBRELLA FOR PAIN

LIFE WAS LIKE a chocolate chip cookie, filled with sweet bites of precious memories, scattered with dark flavored days of misery. As time passed, the beautiful relationship, I once had with my mom slowly began to fade away. Sierra soon became the newest star in my midnight sky, as she helped me change some of my bad habits. Reaching my true potential was the goal, as I became more focused on what I wanted to do in life. Just being around Sierra's family so much, helped me a lot. They showed me what love and compassion looked like while exposing me to new experiences. Incredibly grateful for those moments, I would always make sure I extended my gratitude by just cleaning up my act, as well as, going over to their house every Sunday to cut the grass or help as Sierras' mom cooked dinner. Truth be told, I went over to there get some of her moms' delicious Sunday dinner, cause boy – that woman could cook.

Feeling good about things, my hopes were high for the future that awaited me. My plans were to become a forensic scientist because I wanted to help bring closure to families of unsolved murder cases within my city. It was an all too familiar story from my neighborhood, so I figured this would be the best career for me, especially knowing that I could make a difference in this cruel world.

Getting prepared to go outside so I could catch up with my boys from the neighborhood, my mom came barging through my bedroom door, damn near breaking the door off the hinges. She screamed while throwing something at me, "What the hell is this doing in your room?"

Ducking to avoid being hit by the object she threw, I nervously replied, "What are you talking about ma? I ain't do nothing," as I panned my eyes around the room to see what she had thrown at me. "What the hell I told your ass about bringing that shit in my house? Get your shit, and the get the hell out of my house, NOW!" She yelled.

Continuing my search, I pleaded, "What was it ma? I ain't do nothing I promise." But she just stood there and yelled, "Shut yo lying ass up. I'm just about sick of you and your damn bullshit boy. You always think I'm playing with your ass but I'ma show you how much I'm playing with your ass today."

For the life of me, I could not find the object she had thrown, until I shook the sheets on my bed and a small bag of weed came flying onto the floor. I picked it up suspiciously and replied, "Ma, this not mine." But immediately, she rejected my response by saying, "Well, if it ain't yours, then how the hell did it get in your room?"

Hearing those words, my only reaction was to close my eyes and keep my mouth shut because I knew exactly how it got in here. Picking the small baggy up, I attempted to hand it over to my mom while saying, "Ma, I swear this ain't mine. I ain't never bring any weed in your house ma; I put that on everything."

It was as if she didn't hear a word I was saying because right after I said that, she replied, "You think I'm stupid? I know you and them no good ass lil boys you be hanging with, call y'all self's some so-called goddam 'drug dealers.' Uhm hmm, Gary told me how one of your lil dumbass homeboys said that you were supposed to be involved with it.

"Watch, keep playing and your lil dumbass going to end up dead or sitting in the back seat of somebody police car just like the rest of your lil dumbass friends and if the police do catch your ass, I'ma make sure I tell them to keep you. So, yo ass bet not even think about calling me to come get you, cause I'ma let your ass sit in there until you figure out how stupid yo ass is."

Listening to her talk to me like this wasn't anything new but the real issue I was having, was that the weed she threw at me wasn't mine. I knew it wasn't mine because I stop selling that shit and not once did I ever disrespect her house by bringing it in here. I already knew how she'd react if she found out I had weed in her house but at this moment, she swore me down that it was mine.

"Ma, I'm serious this ain't mine," I said. But she already had her mind made up as she told me, "By the time I get back from using the bathroom, your shit better be packed up, and you better be ready to head out the door." Frustrated that she wouldn't listen to me, I kicked the closet door, sending her right into another round of verbal attacks.

"Oh, so you out here kicking doors and shit in my house? As a matter of fact, pack your shit up now so you can get the hell out of my house. I don't know where the hell you think you at but you done lost your goddamn mind," she shrieked. "But ma, that ain't mine," I cried out in an attempt to get her to believe me and listen to me.

"I'm not trying to hear that shit boy, I done gave your ass one too many chances, and this is the last draw. You got to go, so get your shit so you can get out my damn house. I don't care where you go, but your ass can't stay here." Trying to convince her that I was telling the truth, I walked towards her crying, "Ma please, I love you - don't do this. I promise you this ain't mine," but she didn't care as she pushed me away.

Hearing the commotion going on in my room, Gary walked up saying, "Yo, what the hell y'all making all this goddamn noise in the house for? I know y'all see the baby trying to sleep." That's when my mama said, "His lil dumb ass had weed in his room after I been told his as that he had one more time to try me before he had to go."

With the stupid look he always had on his face, Gary responded, "Well then, make him get his shit and leave then." That's when my mood instantly shifted, from being hurt to one of disgust. I couldn't believe that this dude walked up in here and was going to let me take the blame for a bag of weed that wasn't mine.

Losing my cool, I blurted out, "Ma this ain't mine this Gary's. You know he smokes in the house all the time. Did you even think to ask him?" And before you knew she was throwing her fist at me and yelling, "Who in the hell do you think you talking to boy? I will beat your ass in this house boy, don't you play with me."

Chiming in Gary said, "And don't be putting my name in shit. That ain't got nothing to do with me. I been told your ass to stop acting like you were hard out here in these streets with your lil soft ass. So, get your shit and get out this damn house before I put you out my damn self." After he said that, the only thing he did was add more fuel to the already burning sensation of chaos rising inside of me.

Without realizing it, I shouted, "Man shut yo ass up. Damn, I'm tired of you always trying me as if I'm one of these busters you be out here playing with in the streets. I'll punch you in your shit." Angered by my words, he pushed pass my mama, knocking her into the door, nearly causing her to fall. Gary charged me and grabbed me by my throat as shoved me backward and pinned me against the wall.

Cheering him on, my mom yelled out, "Beat his has Gary. Beat his ass." Spitting on my face from the excessive talking he was doing, he said, "I'll beat your lil ass in this house boy. I don't know who the hell you think you talking to." With my airway restricted by the immense pressure he was applying to my throat, I replied, "Well do it then, you soft ass punk. You always want to pick on somebody smaller than you." And before you know it, his fist came slamming into my stomach, knocking the wind right out of me.

My eyes dilated, as I dropped to the floor, holding my hand against my stomach gasping for air. Everything started to move in slow motion; their voices began to sound distorted, as I could hear him say to me, "Now get your punk ass up and get the hell out of this house." Dizzy and trying to maintain consciousness, I could see my mom standing there with her arms folded and looking at me in disgust.

Helpless, I struggled to crawl on top of my bed. Still holding my stomach, I laid down crying until I regained energy because to me - this shit wasn't over yet. I'd be damned if I was just going to let this asshole punch me in the stomach and get away with it. To make matters worse, my mom stood there and encouraged him to do this. Naw, they both had me messed up because I damn sure wasn't about to let any of this fly.

I began to tremble from the intense anger festering within. Packing all my things into a black trash bag and a few pillow cases, I sat on the edge of my bed once I was done. With my head down and in between my lap, I cried as the thought of having to leave made me feel sick. Even though we had always gone through some tough times, things never got this bad.

But as I began to think about what just happened to me, resentment overpowered me and the idea of killing Gary saturated my thoughts. I picked my head up, got off the bed and stood in front of the mirror connected to my dresser. At this point, all I could see was the face of anger, and I needed to show Gary better than I could tell him after punching me in my stomach.

Standing in the hallway, I could see him sitting in the living room watching TV as my mom took a shower. I played it over and over in my head about how this would end up. But for me, I knew that my next move had to happen no matter what. So, I quietly walked into the kitchen, reached into the cabinet and pulled out two cans of beans. Lighting flashed on the outside of the window as the groggy ambiance of thunder followed.

Hurrying back to my room, I stared into the abyss, as rain drops pounded against my bedroom window. With every moment passing, it seemed like the rain was pouring harder and the thunder grew louder. Finally, I heard my mom turning off the water to the shower, and I knew this was about to be it. I walked back into the hallway and stood there watching Gary, who was clueless of my stalker-like behavior.

That's when my mom opened the bathroom door and saw that I was standing in the dark hallway with a can of beans in my hand. With a towel wrapped around her body, she said to me, "Didn't I tell your ass to be gone a long time ago? I don't give a damn if it's raining outside, you better find an umbrella and get your ass out my house." I looked over to my left and what did I see? I saw the face of a mother who had no respect for me, and with the viciousness of a lion stalking a gazelle in the African Safari, I darted into the living room towards Gary.

Locked on my target, I raised the can of beans and with all my might, crashed down on Gary's' skull, sending blood spewing everywhere. He screamed in horror, as I hit him repeatedly and he attempted to push me away. But I had no remorse, as my mom pleaded for me to stop before she ran over to grab her cellphone to call the police.

Blood gushed from the top of Gary's left eye, as I continued to throw a fury of haymakers before he picked me up and slammed me to the floor. As he tried to fight back, he busted my lip open right before I kicked him in the balls. I managed to crawl away from him and ran right out of the front door.

The sound of lightning crackled in the distance as I

stood behind Gary's car. With the other can of beans that I had, I slung it as hard has as I could at his car. Shattering the entire back window of his car into a thousand pieces. I was getting soaked by the rain, so, I took off running as fast as I could down the street before they came outside.

The rain felt like small grains of rice thumping against my face, as I ran for dear life. I couldn't tell you how far I ran, but when I saw an entrance to a city park, I dashed through it and hid underneath the cover of a playground slide. I dropped underneath it and began to ball in tears, as my soul no longer felt worthy of being a part of this world.

Hyperventilating, I cried for a while, until my throat became sore, my mind become aloof, and my eyes gazed upon a world of nothingness. Sitting there alone, I fell into a dark pit of grief, knowing that no one would be searching for me. But without warning, I noticed a familiar voice calling out to me. "DJ, where you at?" it said. But motionless and out of touch with my surroundings, I didn't bother to respond.

As the rain continued to thump against the domed covering, I heard the voice call out again, "Aye yo, DJ, where you at bruh? I know you out here." Still, I remained unresponsive and unconcerned with whoever was trying to reach me. I was too busy trying to bring myself to terms with what I had done.

Then the sound of footsteps grew closer to me, and the voice whispered, "Yo DJ? That's you?" Drifting in and out of my impending daze, I turned my head to see Chad standing next to me. I couldn't help but wonder, "Why he was here and how did he even find me?"

"Yo DJ, you alright man? I heard the police out here looking for you because something happened at your crib, so I came looking for you. At first, I thought about checking at your folk's crib, but I figured you wouldn't go there. You good bruh, everything good at the crib?"

The aching of my tender soul couldn't bear another word, so I closed my eyes and tried to let go of the world before me. Falling asleep to the mist of rain droplets spraying my body, I realized that indeed I was living in a selfish and undesirable world, but at least Chad was here to reassure me that I wasn't always alone.

CHAPTER 9

Near the Shoreline

HAVE YOU EVER listened to the peaceful sound of waves as they collided with sand resting on the shore of a beach? They begin by forming an unprecedented roar from as far away as the eyes can see. The momentum it transports pushes all-natural possessions clear of its path, as it sets its sights on reaching the shore. With every roll, they bring howls of the oceanic symphony that intensifies with the reverberation of its call, causing the distance between them and the shoreline to gradually decline. They rise and fall amidst octaves, hoping to bring forth a finely tuned note that plays a crisp song to your liking. The mountainous waves are vehemently collapsing into the next, creating a monument of uncertainty that is derived from a place unknown. You stand there observing with your feet in the sand as the choir of the wind and sea birds sing along to the rhythmic tune. Your mind slowly comes to ease, your heart begins to breathe, and your ears grow wide as the fizzing of what was once a roaring wave, soothes your soul beneath your feet.

The day of the fight, my mom had called the cops on me but decided not to press charges because she knew they had provoked me. I ended up sleeping in the park that night, trembling in my sleep as the howling of the brisk wind kept waking me up. Walking past my mom's house, I could see that all my things were sitting outside on the front porch.

I headed to my grandmothers, and when I got there, I told her about everything that happened the day before. Upset, she said to me, "Ain't no way on heaven's green earth, would I have ever let a man put his hands on my child. There ain't no way that he and I would have ever been together after that. I just don't understand how she would even encourage him to do that to you. I am so sorry that you had to go through that baby, but I been telling them your mama got a few screws loose.

"I saw it a long time ago when your daddy used to bring her around here, and she would act like she couldn't eat or didn't want to talk to nobody. I always told your daddy, I would say to him, 'Now Derrick. You decided to be with this young lady Bri or Red or whatever y'all want to call her, so if you get her pregnant you going to have to deal with whatever she gives you because that's the decision you made.'"

Grandma Diana was always spitting some knowledge to me, and somehow, she always believed in me, even when I didn't believe in my damn self. She was always trying to get me to go to church but the way I was living and the people surrounding me, I didn't see how the church was going to help me.

Besides, all them pastors in the hood do is take people money and buy themselves fancy clothes, while stunting on all these broke church folks with their brand-new cars. I couldn't understand how there were so many churches on every corner, yet there are still more killings in the hood than at a beef slaughterhouse or "Why none of these churches had programs that helped families of victims from these senseless killings or free programs that educated youth on life other than religion?" So, in my mind, I had to look out for myself and myself only.

As usual, I always felt good after talking to my Grandma Dee. Seeing that I looked dirty and my clothes were still damp, she allowed me to take a shower and gave me some of my dad's old clothes to put on, that she still had hanging around in the house. Soon after she filled my stomach with some of her good ole cooking, so we sat and talked for a bit. When we were done, I got up and walked over to this shelf where my grandma had pictures of the family. I saw an old picture of my old boy when he was a kid and saw how much we reassembled each other. Out of nowhere, Liyah crept up behind me and said, "Yup boy, you sure do look just like your daddy, don't you?" as I stared at the photo.

Placing the picture back onto the shelf, I replied, "I ain't got no daddy." That's when Liyah, snatched me by the wrist, turning me around and said angrily, "Boy don't you ever let me her say something as stupid as that ever again, you hear me? Your daddy loved you, and he was a good man.

"I know he would've given up anything in the world just to be here with you right now to watch you grow up. It's not his fault that the Lord called upon him when he did, but you got to understand that your daddy would've done everything he could just to make sure that you were happy. So, don't be mad at him, just be thankful because there's a lot of other kids in this world that don't even have a clue as to who their daddy is or even their mama."

Lowering my head down in pity, Liyah placed her hand on my chin and lifted my head. She then looked me in the eyes and told me, "DJ, you are becoming a man now. So, you must make sure you are making the right decisions in life. Ain't nobody going to babysit you or hold your hand like you want them to, be grateful for life." She said, before pulling me in, hugging me tightly, to tell me how much she loved me.

Shortly after I left Grandma Dee house, I headed out to my aunty Shay's crib. It was humid outside, and the atmosphere felt sticky as I walked down the street to the nearby bus stop. My aunty had to move when someone bought the old place she was renting and raised the rent way above her available income.

When I finally got there, I rang the doorbell a few times before Aunty Shay finally opened the door. Furiously, she said, "DJ, where in the hell your ass been, boy? We have been looking for your ass all damn day. What in the hell were you thinking, putting your goddam hands on your mama?"

"Put my hands on my mama?" I said abruptly, before looking down and mumbling, "She always lying me on me man. I swear I can't stand that lady dawg, her or that stupid ass dude Gary."

"Uh hello," my aunty said to me, "You better watch your damn mouth. I know you see me standing here. Now, I don't know what you got going on but you not about to bring whatever it is over here with you."

Staring at my aunty with the face of innocence, I delicately said, "I'm sorry Aunty, it's just that she always lying on me. You know I ain't put my hands on my mama. I promise I ain't touch her Aunty, that's on everything I love." She stood there for a second just looking at me with suspicion in her eyes before asking, "What the hell are you doing fighting Gary for anyway? He a grown ass man, you don't pay any bills in that house.

"I don't care what he said to you; you should've just ignored it and let it go. When you get your own place, then you can have a say to what you will and will not do, but until then, that's your mama house and no matter how much you don't like Gary you got to respect the fact that he's your mama baby daddy and who she chose to be with."

It was apparent that she wasn't told the truth about the situation, so I went ahead and explained to her that the only reason any of this even happened was that he punched me in the stomach, as I showed her the bruise on my ribs. I told her every detail, from the start to the finish of how I ended up breaking the car window. She could see that my side of the story was making a lot more sense than the one she was told yesterday.

Waving her hand for me to come inside of the house she fumed with disappointment. I walked inside and promptly fell on her couch, closing my eyes as the cold air circulated in the room. "Why didn't you call me yesterday or at least leave when she told you to?" Aunty asked. "Because I knew it wasn't mine, she just didn't want to listen to me," I replied while scooting myself upright on the sofa. "But when Gary came at me sideways and hit me in the stomach, honestly, I just blanked out."

Rubbing her forehead with her left hand on her hip, she sighed and said, "I don't know what's wrong with your mama." I could only hold my head down as I thought to myself the same exact thing. Then I asked, "Aye, Aunty she kicked me out, and as I walked by the house today, I saw all my stuff on the front porch, you think I can stay with you?"

Taking a moment to respond, she said, "I don't know DJ, you ain't about to be having nobody running in and out of my house all day and if you do you going to need to get yourself a job." Excited because although she was a bit doubtful of me staying over, she didn't exactly say 'No.' I replied, "Trust me, Aunty, nobody will even know that I'm over here. Plus, I can get a job that way I can help you pay the rent and stuff."

She replied, "I don't need you to help me pay my bills, you going to need a job for you because I don't want you around here asking me for money every time you go broke." I laughed before saying, "I ain't never broke Aunty, but please, I'll cook, clean, do whatever you need me to do just as long as I can stay here with you. I ain't got nowhere else to go."

With a smile on her face, she said, "Boy you think I was going to let you be stuck out on the streets, you're my only nephew." I leaped for joy, running over to hug her. "That's why I love you, Aunty Shay, you're my favorite," I said. "Yeah, yeah DJ I know," she said, as I smothered her with love. "Now let me go, so I can call your mama and let her know I'm coming over to pick up your stuff up."

"Okay Aunty, but you think I can use your house phone, so I can call my girlfriend and tell her what happened?" I asked. She looked at me with a mischievous smile and said, "Girlfriend? What lil girl let you trick them into dating you?" I responded, "Haha I see you got jokes, Aunty."

The level of comfort I got by staying with my aunty was indescribable. I didn't have my own room, but the sofa in the living room was enough for me. I was used to sleeping like this anyway. Being there, it brought me back to the bittersweet moment when Mama and I lived with her for a short period, before she kicked us out.

When she found out why I had been kicked out, it somehow made Sierra and I got a lot closer. By this time, we had officially started dating and made things a lot clearer about where we were heading with this relationship. She was my motivation and hope in this garden of despair. I knew that with her by my side everything would be alright because she was the second closest person to me next to my boy Chad.

Coming home after school one day, Sierra and I stopped by to get some ice cream with the new car her parents bought her. As goofy and playful as she was, this girl took a huge lick from my ice cream when the guy handed it to me. Talking about, "What's yours is mine, and what's mine is mine." I pretended to be upset, but all I could do was smile and shake my head because I loved her playful personality.

Hopping in the car, the two of us headed to my Aunty's crib when one of our favorite songs came on. Singing loudly and laughing we both enjoyed each other's smile until we hit the corner and saw an ambulance parked outside of my aunty Shay's, house along with people standing around on the sidewalk being nosey. Immediately,

I told Sierra, "Hurry up," as I turned the music down so that I could see clearer.

Pulling up, I hopped out of the car before Sierra could even put the car park in and ran through the fenced gate towards the front door. I came to an abrupt halt, once I approached the opening of the door. I saw my aunty Shay laying on the couch with an oxygen mask on her face and two paramedics standing by her.

In a whimpering cry, I slowly walked towards them and asked, "Aunty, what's going on? What happened?" In a scratchy voice she said, "DJ, I'm okay. I just called the ambulance because I couldn't breathe. Everything is fine, they just going to take me to the hospital to make sure I'm alright."

It was impossible for me to register that she was okay because if she were, then there'd be no need for them to take her to the hospital. Moments later Sierra walked through the door and slightly screamed, thinking that my aunty Shay was dead. She ran up to me and grabbed hold of my arm, as she said, "DJ, what's wrong with Aunty? Is she okay? What are they doing to her?"

I could only stare into my Aunty's eyes, as she smiled at me with the oxygen mask on her face, attempting to reassure us that everything was okay. They eventually rolled a stretcher inside of the house to carry her to the ambulance. Melting on the inside, I remained calm - trying to keep my cool so that Sierra wouldn't freak out. One of the medics told us that it would be okay if we came to the hospital if we liked.

Sitting in the waiting room of the hospital, Sierra held onto my arm, as she leaned laid her head on my shoulder. We waited anxiously for Aunty Shay to be discharged from the hospital. A million and one things raced through my mind, as I attempted to put together the pieces that would answer the question: "Why she couldn't breathe?" I knew that she had gotten a bad cold, but I was certain that a cold wasn't the reason for this. I sunk my head on top of Sierras' and hoped that it wasn't what I thought it was. I just had a bad feeling that there was a chance Aunty Shay might've had cancer.

It took nearly two hours before a doctor came out and instructed us to follow him into the room where my aunty Shay was being held. Seeing her lying in that hospital bed, I held back the waterfall of tears building in my eyes. She smiled at me the entire time as I walked up. Standing next to the bed, she grabbed my hand as Sierra wiped the tears flowing from my eyes.

Nephew, I got something to tell you, she said while straining to talk. Speechless and worried at the same time, I could only respond with a meager, "Yes, Aunty." I could tell whatever she was getting ready to say was going to be bad, so she closed her eyes, taking a deep gulp of air with tears running down her face. In desperation, I asked, "Aunty what they say? You alright, right?"

Looking at me with tears flooding from her eyes, she responded, "Yes. I'm alright DJ but," she said with a pause, as her hand began to shake vigorously while holding onto mine. "But what, Aunty?" I replied. Bracing myself to hear the devastating news of her cancerous diagnosis, she licked a tear from the side of her lip and said to me slowly, "DJ I have AIDS."

Startled by her words, I shook my head and said "Naw, Aunty. That ain't right. They messed up or something, I'ma tell them they got to redo these tests. They got the wrong results, let me go get the doctor." Gripping my arm as I turned around, she pulled me back towards her.

"DJ, don't! Come here. I'm okay nephew, so you don't have to worry." I couldn't help it as I started to cry uncontrollably, forcing Sierra to wrap her arms around my body attempting to comfort me. "This ain't right Aunty. This shit ain't right. They can't be lying to us like this man," I said as I fell into a pool of sorrow.

"Listen to me," she said, with her face even more intense than before. "It's going to be okay DJ," she said to me again, but I could only shake my head in sheer disbelief. "I've been living with this sickness for as long as you been alive DJ. I got it from Jaleel's father. He was out cheating on me with other women while I was pregnant and somehow, I managed to get it myself. But I thank God that when Jaleel was born, he wasn't infected like I was. He was just as healthy as can be, the doctors told me he was a miracle baby because the chances of that happening were rare.

"So, like I said, I do not want you to worry about me. I take my medication every day, but sometimes this happens. My body can't always fight off the sickness, so I get a little sicker than I usually am sometimes. They going to keep me overnight or for a few days until I get better but don't you worry about nothing because I'ma be home in no time DJ, you hear me?"

Blindsided by this, my comprehension of this was still short of unclear because Aunty looked damn healthy to me. I never saw her down, or whenever she did get sick, she would sleep it off and in no time, be right back to normal. I was a mess because if I lost her, I didn't know what I would do.

Before leaving the hospital, Sierra called her parents and asked if they would allow me to come over and spend the night at their place because she didn't want me to sleep alone. Sleeping in their living room that night, I stared into space, as the overwhelming thoughts of my life ran across the ceiling, while I silently cried myself to sleep.

CHAPTER 10

Desolate Catacombs

IRONING MY CLOTHES in an empty house, I could feel the pressure of the universe as it attempted to dismantle my sense of hope. It was going to be my fourth interview in two weeks, and I had a bad feeling that I wasn't about to get this job. Aunty Shay had been doing better, since her last visit to the hospital but things weren't the same anymore. I found myself worrying about her so much, that I could hardly focus at school. Taking fewer hours at work, she was struggling to make ends meet, and it caused me to feel as though I was a walking failure because I had nothing to bring to the table. I didn't want to get back to selling weed, but for some reason, it seemed like the only possible thing I could do to help. Believing I wasn't going to get the job, I stopped ironing my pants and decided not to go to the interview. Making up my mind, I knew what I needed to do and working forty hours a week for minimum wage wasn't going to cut it for me. I needed to get some money now.

Heading to the streets, I put on my mask of toughness as I looked forward to seeing my old homies. I was expecting them to be happy since I hadn't been around in a while. But as I approached them at a dice game, they all seemed nonchalant when they dapped me up asking me, If I had finally gotten rid of Sierra because she was making me soft.

Knowing how they joked around, I didn't take offense to it. I knew that was their way of expressing how they missed having me around. Chopping it up with my boy Cam, who was now running things, I asked him, "Aye Cam. I need you to put me back on to some work. You think you can handle that for me?"

Licking his lips and looking around Cam replied, "Ha, Naw man. I don't know what you talking about bruh?" Baffled by his statement, I replied, "Man stop playing bruh. I need you to put me back on; I'm trying to get back on my feet dawg." He looked at me while rubbing his hands together and said, "Naw bruh, not today." Thinking that he literally meant not 'Today,' I said, "Well, smooth then. When you think you going to have it ready for me?"

Anticipating a date from him, he then replied, "Ha-you don't get it bruh, you been gone from the streets way too long. The game ain't the same as it used to be. I can't put you on." Startled by what I heard from Cam, I replied angrily, "What the hell you mean you can't put me on? Am I not the one that put you in the game? If it weren't for me, you wouldn't even be out here."

Stepping into my chest with his fist balled up, he said, "Yo, who you think you talking to? I ain't that trick Sierra. So, I suggest you get your ass of this block before you get your ass whooped," as he pointed his finger at my chest.

Feeling tested, I responded, "Well do something then, you soft ass buster," as we both stood with our foreheads against one another's before I shoved him out of my face. "Exactly! Just like I thought," I said, "You already know what's up, but I see how it is now. Slimes grow some balls over the weekend, and suddenly, they forget who was there with them from the jump. It's all good Cam, you always been a crab anyway."

Hearing our heated conversation, some random new dude to the block pulled out his gun and pointed it in my face saying, "Man, you better tighten up fool before you get left stanking out here on this sidewalk." That's when Cam yelled at him, "Man put that shit down before you get your ass beat." The guy replied, "Naw Cam. This fool trying you and you already know I'm bout that life. I'll handle his ass for you right now, just tell me what's up."

Repeating himself, Cam ordered the idiot to put the gun down as he pulled out his gun and began to point it at the dudes' head. Disoriented, he looked at Cam and said, "Yo, what you pulling your gun out on me for?" Capturing the seriousness Cam expressed on his face, dude lowered his gun and walked away whispering something slick as he stared at me with a mean mugging.

"Look bruh, I see you been doing good and shit in school, but right now this ain't where you need to be," Cam said to me. "Keep looking for a part time job or something bruh. Hell, cut grass or wash cars if you got to but I see you changing for the better, and as your 'Brother' I can't let you throw that shit away for this. Here go three hundred dollars. Shit ain't much, but it's enough to help you with something.

"What we do over here ain't nothing compared to what you got going on bruh. You got a good girl; you figured that school shit out, plus you always been that dude, so I know you're going to be straight. The only thing we look forward to over here is: who gon' to get shot, who gon' kill somebody or who going to jail first. You don't want no parts of this man, I'm telling you.

"The grass ain't greener on this side bruh. It's all screwed up and filled with dudes who will call you brother one minute but in the next, try to set you up or be the one smashing your girl behind your back. So, listen, you got out of this shit for a reason, and you'll be a damn fool to get back in it."

I couldn't reject what he was saying because deep down, that was exactly how I felt. Personally, I didn't want to get sucked back into that life, but shit, it was the only way I knew I could make a good amount of money in a short amount of time. Thankful for Cam and what he told me, I dapped him up as we agreed that we were still brothers for life.

Being that it was the middle of senior year, I had to figure out what my next move was and figure it out real soon. Aunty still had random episodes that caused her to head to the hospital, and I still hadn't found a job. Talking with Sierra, she convinced me that I needed to see my guidance counselor because she wanted me to plan and explore my options of going to college. I swear, sometimes this girl swore she was my mama instead of my girlfriend.

Sierra had scheduled the meeting for me when I met with this counselor named Ms. Evans. When I got to her office, she asked me questions about what schools I wanted to go to after graduating and what type of degrees I wanted to pursue. With my mind on other things, I wasn't thinking about going to college that often, so I couldn't give her a straight up answer.

Seeing that I wasn't taking the meeting serious, Ms. Evans took a deep breath and said, "You know what son, how about you tell me something interesting about yourself? Talk to me about who you are. What it is that you enjoy? Or anything else that we can come up with." I didn't want to be there, plus I wasn't about to start expressing myself to a stranger. So, I hit her with the superficial things like; my favorite color, favorite foods and just a bunch of other things that had nothing to do with the reason I was in her office.

Giving me an evil look because she knew I was bullshitting, Ms. Evans said to me, "Listen. Stop messing around trying to tell me things that you think I want to hear. Talk to me about you, and I mean the real you. And stop slouching in my chair, sit upright and act like you got some sense in here."

Without hesitation, I unwillingly lifted myself upright in that seat because I could sense that she wasn't about to continue playing games with me. She then said, "Now again, tell me about yourself. I want to know the real you and not the one you think you are."

Rubbing my eyes, I responded, "Naw Ms. E., I thought I came in here to talk about college and stuff, not about me," as I attempted to laugh it off, so I didn't sound disrespectful. But she stared at me with a blank look on her face, still waiting for me to participate. Caressing my scalp with my fingers, I was gradually grew uncomfortable because I wanted to talk to her but I just didn't know if I could trust her. So, in one last attempt to avoid the conversation I said, "You sure you want to know about me? Like, who I really am?"

"Yes," she said to me in a very tranquil voice, "Just let your mind flow and allow your heart to say whatever it needs to say." Taking a deep breath, I began to talk to Ms. Evans about the person she wanted to know. I mentioned to her that the pain of my life that came with trying to cope with the death of so many family members, as well as, having to deal with Gary and feeling like my mama had given up on me.

With her elbows propped on her desk, she sat there and listened to every word that I had to say until I ended with, "I bet Sierra told you to ask me these questions." Replying in confirmation, she confidently said, "Yes sir, Sierra did ask me to talk to you because she felt like you needed someone to talk to other than her. I know you may not always like talking to people about how you feel but the more you bottle up those emotions inside of you, the more you start to feel bad about life. So sometimes you got to talk to people to feel better.

"But you see, life itself is much like driving a car early in the morning with a thick cloud of fog covering the entire road. It's almost impossible to see where you're going and sometimes you can't even see the cars driving right in front of you. We continue to drive through that fog because at that moment all we have is our "faith" to guide us.

"Yea we may pump the brakes a few times or slow down so that we don't crash, but still we continue to drive forward without a doubt. See, that's what life is like sometimes, so you can't let the fog of life's disappointments stop you from reaching your destinations. You go to push through it all with faith, that somehow - someway, you will accomplish all the things you desire.

"I know what you are thinking; I'm just trying to preach to you about life just like everybody else tries to. But listen, If I honestly didn't care about helping you live up to the true potential I see within you. You better believe I wouldn't have even allowed you to come into my office and waste my time today."

Observing the powerful words, she spoke, I lowered my head in shame because I couldn't believe I allowed myself to become this lost over all these years. I had drifted into a place of no return, and here I was every day, fighting a battle between who I was and who I thought I should be. I asked her, "Ms. E, when you look at me, like, what do you see in me?"

To her surprise, she smiled because she was happy that I was trying to engage in a deeper conversation. She replied, "Well, I'll tell you this for sure. I can see right through that ugly little mask you wear, trying to show everybody how tough you are. You don't have to act tough all the time. It's okay for a man to feel grief, love and even express joy.

"You are a strong black man, and I want you to understand that you can do whatever it is that you put your mind to. I know that you are far more capable of doing something greater with your life than you can even believe yourself. Think about this for a second - you have gone through all of these experiences and look at you, you're still standing. That's what I see when I look at you. A young African King with a million dreams and a sharp mind that will help him get there. Especially with a brilliant young African Queen-like Sierra right by your side. You just have to believe it yourself."

Listening to Ms. Evans, gave me chills because I'd never met a stranger to speak of me in such a manner. With my eyes sort of tearing up, she looked at me and said, "The most important question for yourself would be. When you're looking in the mirror, who is it that you see?"

With the complete honesty of my heart I responded, "To be real Ms. E, I don't even know." Reassuring me, she said, "No great civilization was built in a day, and no one is born knowing what their role in life is. It takes time for us to mature and figure out who we really are, so don't worry yourself too much because I think you'll know the answer to that question in due time."

Inspired and pleased that she had taken the time out of her busy day to speak to me. I ventured into a new conversation by saying, "So, Ms. E, you think I can go to college and become a Forensic Scientist?" Without any uncertainty, she replied, "Well, of course, you can. Let's go ahead and pull up your transcripts to see what your current grade point average is. This way we can start considering schools you can apply to."

Grinning from cheek-to-cheek, I replied, "You know I'm going to be the best looking Forensic Scientist out there, right?" She looked over at me, peeping from the top of her classes and said, "Boy please." Jokingly, I responded, "But I'm for real though. Watch! You're going to see me looking clean when I pull up to these crime scenes." But in the midst of me talking, I could see her face turning bitter as she stared intensely at her computer screen.

"If it's about those service hours, I already started knocking them," I said. "No, I don't think it's just that," she replied. Feeling unsettled, I leaned forward to gain clarity by asking, "You mean to tell me, I got something else to do?" Gently, Ms. Evans responded, "Well from what I see here. It looks like, when you were in the ninth and tenth grade, you failed a few classes but never went to night school or summer school to make them up. So, from the looks of it, you might not be able to graduate just yet. But I can figure this out for you."

"Wait! Hold on; you mean to tell that I'm no got to graduate on time?" Looking at me with the face of regret she said, "Yes, but it's going to be okay. Stuff like this happens all the time. You can walk at graduation, but you'll just need to finish the rest of those classes at an adult education program to get your official diploma. You can still go to college; you'll just have to enroll once you finish the program." Placing my hand on my face and leaning my elbow on my knee, my mood quickly shifted.

Attempting to comfort me she put her hand on my arm, but I quickly snatched away and stood up. "How y'all just now telling me this? All this time y'all knew this. Had me thinking that I was about to graduate and now you want to tell me I got to make up some classes to get my diploma. Man, that's some bull."

"Listen, sit down. It's not as bad as you think it is, she said to calm me down. But feeling betrayed, I walked out of her office and headed back to class. For the rest of the day, I remained silent, listening to classmates discuss their plans for homecoming and what colleges they were applying to. Overwhelmed by everything, I eventually stood up and walked out of the classroom because I couldn't tolerate hearing them talk about everything that I'd been hoping for.

When school ended, instead of riding home with Sierra like always, I decided that I was going to walk. I needed some time to myself, just to breathe and clear my mind. As I walked north up Seventh Avenue, I was overwhelmed with anger and disappointment, when I heard a car honking its horn at me. I turned to see what their problem was, but it was Sierra yelling, "Get in the car. Where are you going? I was looking for you."

"Just leave me alone and go home Sierra," I said, not wanting to be bothered now. "DJ, get in the car. I know you see this traffic building up behind me," she yelled out, as cars honked their horns in frustration before speeding around her.

Realizing that I wasn't about to get in the car, she mashed on the gas and pulled onto the opening of the sidewalk to cut me off. "Get in the car," she said one last time, trying to be commanding with her squeaky voice. But I just walked around the car with my hands in my pocket.

I heard her sigh loudly as she put the car in park, unbuckled her seatbelt and got out to come after me. Walking up from behind, she grabbed hold of my arm pulling my left hand out of my pocket. "Babe, what's wrong with you? Why are you acting like this? Why are you ignoring me?" she asked in a concerned voice. I replied, "Nothing, Sierra. It's not you, just leave me alone. I need some time to myself to think."

Sierra wasn't the kind of girl to just leave things alone without an answer, she was persistent and was going to make sure she tried whatever she could to get me to talk to her. "Was it something I said to you?" she asked. "No Sierra, it wasn't you. Dang, I just told you this, so can you let me go, please? I don't want to talk about it." But she wouldn't let go, as she tightened her grip on my arm causing her nails to lightly pinched my skin.

"Please talk to me," she said in a serious yet pleading tone. "Alright Sierra, just let my arm go," I replied irritably. "Okay, so tell me what's wrong," Sierra said again, curious to know what was bothering me. Taking a deep breath, I said to her, "I'm not graduating."

Staring at me with a puzzled face, she replied, "What do you mean you're not graduating?" I then yelled, "I played around in the ninth and tenth grade failing some classes. So now I don't have enough credits, and I'm not going to graduate. You happy? You got what you wanted - I'm not as smart as you thought I was, so just leave me alone and let me go."

"Wait, is that what Ms. Evans told you?" she said to me. As I walked over to lean on a nearby fence, I began to cry as I replied, "Yes. That's what she told me. I feel so stupid. All my hard work, trying to keep my grades up, staying out of trouble - doing all of that so I could do something better with my life and now I can't even graduate. I swear this shit ain't fair man."

"DJ! Don't cry; it's going to be okay baby. I'm sure there's something we can do about this, we'll figure it out," Sierra said to me, as she wiped away my tears. "There ain't no way, what part don't you understand? This shit is done with. I can't get no job, I'm not going to graduate, like I don't even know what the hell I'm even alive for man," I responded while continuing to sob on her shoulder.

"Let's go home DJ," she said, as she held me tightly while holding on to me as we walked towards the passenger side of her car. The drive back to her place was silent, as I leaned back in the seat and stared out of the car window. Just gazing upon the world that never seemed to care or even recognize my mere existence.

CHAPTER 11

GREY SKY

N O MATTER HOW bad we attempt to escape the stresses of life, they never let up on stalking you. For some odd reason, I would always catch myself looking over my shoulders, feeling as though something was watching me or walking behind me as I walked the unpleasant streets of Liberty City. The echoing sounds of guns shot filled the air with a bad tune of catastrophic fate, which always left you wondering if it was someone that you knew being gunned down or another innocent bystander, in the right place at the wrong time. My sanity was on the brink of failure and heading for self-destruction as each day passed. Feeling purposeless, I slowly began to care less about the cruel world I was living in, which I felt only intended to box me up and ship me off to my imminent demise. I tried my best to hold on to what sanity I had left but with drugs altering my perception of reality, the hue of the blue skies soon became undesirably pale.

Drugs and alcohol had become my best friends, as I looked forward to finding a peace of mind every time we met. It was something weird about smoking, that put me in a realm of high intensity, which created extreme levels of unwanted paranoia but somehow at the same time, it allowed me to forget about all the dumb shit that was going on in my life.

Getting high eventually put a strain on the relationship I had with Sierra but there was nothing comparable to the amount of ease it gave my soul. I didn't care how much she annoyed me to stop; I just felt like I had listened to her for far too long and now I needed to do what felt was best for me.

Senior year had rolled by and left me in the dust. I eventually dropped out of school during the last few months, considering I wasn't going to graduate anyway. Sierra persisted that I went ahead and took that adult education program to complete my high school diploma but already set with her plans to go off the college, I didn't want to hear anything from her. The people at the program said that it would end up taking another year instead of a few months to complete the program. So, I said screw it and let that dumbass dream of going to college flow right down the drain of hopelessness.

Being that we both had different lives to live, a part of me was jealous of Sierra because she never had to worry about the things I went through. So, I was getting tired of her optimistic attitude about me still being able to go to college. From my perspective, I figured that, if this world wanted me to be successful in life then it wouldn't be setting up booby traps and road blocks every time I tried to take a few steps forward in the right direction.

Growing tired of her uninspiring motivational speeches, the chemistry between Sierra slowly began to fade. Once she left for college, I started hanging out with the fellas again, attempting to make ends meet since I was still jobless. I wasn't completely immersed in the old life I once lived, but like they say, "You are the sum of who you surround yourself with."

So, because I was hanging with homies that loved to talk about hitting licks, smashing different chicks and rolling up blunts all day. Sierra was convinced that I had turned into the same kind of person, as she would call back home every day, aggravating me about my decision to go back and hang out with them.

Frankly, she was right about everything she said, but without her being here and no other way to deal with the things that would come to my mind during the middle of the night, "What else was I supposed to do?" My homies were the only people I knew that could relate to me at the time. Plus, they weren't trying to control the decisions I made as a 'Man.'

Nearing the end of her first semester in college, we had become so distant that we both could feel the animosity in the atmosphere when we met for one of the last times. It was Thanksgiving break for her, and although she had come home a few times before, it was almost a month since we last saw each other.

Things between us were so bad that I'd often ask my aunty to say I wasn't home whenever I didn't feel like talking to her after we'd get into a heated argument. But being the determined person that she was, Sierra would never just allow me to have a moment to breathe on my own. After a while, I began to feel as though she was smothering me and becoming too clingy.

Getting back home from a long drive across the state, I was at home watching TV when Sierra called and told me she was back in town. At first, when her name popped up on my cell phone, I pounded my fist into the chair, wishing that she hadn't called me. I couldn't tolerate that every time we'd get on the phone, somehow, we'd end up arguing about something stupid because she was always insecure and assuming.

Nonchalantly, I answered the phone and said, "Hello?" She quickly responded, "I'm not calling to argue with you and I know we haven't spoken in a while, but since I'm back in town I would like to see you in person because I have something I want to talk to you about." Rolling my eyes and taking an exhaustingly deep sigh, I responded, "Yeah, sure. That's straight." She then replied, "Where are you now? Are you free?"

Defensively I uttered, "Why? What's up?" That's when she said, "I'm free until this afternoon, and I thought I'd come by to see you now before I got busy." Feeling as though she was up to no good and was only trying to come over to convince me to get back together. I reluctantly replied with a lie saying, "Well, right now I'm at my aunty crib but I'm getting ready to leave soon, so if you're going to come over, hurry up because I'm not gon be here for long." Without hesitation, she replied, "Okay, I'll be over there in about ten minutes."

Patiently waiting for her to come, it was close to twenty minutes later when I got another phone call from her. Irritated that she wasn't here, I rudely answered the phone and said, "WHAT!?" Apologizing for having me wait she responded, "I'll be there in like five minutes. I'm sorry, I was talking with my parents about something. Are you still at your aunty house?" I then replied, "Yeah man, I'm still over here." Appearing relieved that I hadn't left, she said, "Okay. I'll be there shortly. I'm like down the street - so you can come outside."

Rudely hanging up the phone right after she made her statement, I put on my flip flops, headed outside and posted up on the sidewalk to wait for her. The sun was shining brightly, and the cold winter wind was blowing so hard, it nearly blew my pants away. That's when I finally saw her pulling around the corner in her silver Toyota Camry.

I stood there with my red gym shorts on and black hoodie, as my legs froze like homemade popsicles. She rolled the window down and yelled, "You can get in." Sluggishly, I walked to the car, opened the door and hopped into the passenger seat. My mindset was to remain calm and not let her persuade to do anything that I didn't want to do. She asked, "Can I get a hug?"

Reaching over to give her a hug, I gave her one of those awkward sideways church hugs. Sierra then asked, "So, how have you been? How's Aunty doing?" Unenthusiastically I replied, "We straight." Slouching her head towards her lap, playing with her fingernails, disappointed with my nonchalant behavior she asked, "So, you're not happy to see me?"

Watching a black cat walk across the middle of the street, I continued with my act and replied, "I mean, it is what it is. I ain't going to stress what ain't supposed to be." I could feel her eyes of sadness, staring at me before she lifted her feet into her seat and turned sideways to face me.

Leaning my head on the passenger window with my eyes closed, I thought to myself, "Of course I miss her. I just don't be having time for her nonsense." That's when I heard crying and sniffling coming from Sierra. Opening my left eye, I peeped over to see what was her problem, as she sat there sobbing out of now where. I figured it was a trap, so I closed my eyes again and allowed her to do her thang.

Almost a minute or two went by before she stopped crying and just stared at me. I panned my eyes around the street trying to find anything on the outside of the car to grab my attention so that I wouldn't have to look at her. That's when she said, "If I tell you something, promise me that you won't get mad." Immediately, and with a swift motion of concern, I turned my head towards her to see what she was talking about.

As her voice cracked from emotion, she said to me, "I want you to say it. Tell me that you won't get mad at me, please." At this point, whatever she was about to say to me captured my undivided attention. So, I rose in the seat, rubbing my hands on my thighs before saying, "Aight, what you got to tell me?" But before she would say it, Sierra insisted that I promised her I wouldn't get mad by saying, "No, I need to hear you say it. Just promise me you won't get mad once I tell you what I need to say."

At this point, she was already getting my blood boiling, and I didn't even know what she was going to say. The first thing that came to mind was, "I know this girl ain't go all the way up to these folks' school just to flunk out." I remember, a while ago, she texted me about how she overslept one of her classes and missed an exam.

Impatiently, I spewed out, "Look, just tell me what you got to say, man. Why you always got to make shit so difficult, damn?" Her face grew weary as she replied, "Because, I just need to know that you won't be upset with me after I tell you." With my heart now thumping like a bass drum and my head feeling itchy, I replied, "Alright Sierra, I won't get mad. Now just tell me what's up because you're starting to piss me off by not saying what you got to say."

Balling into a fistful of tears, she said, "I messed up, and I screwed up bad." Growing increasingly impatient I said, "Yo, alright I'm getting out the car." She quickly grabbed me by the arm as I turned to open the door, hysterically yelling out, "No, please, please. Okay, okay. I'll tell you." Rotating back around towards her, I could see that she was physically trembling, so I wasn't sure if I wanted to know what she had to say anymore.

With her back against the driver's door, her feet folded beneath her as she faced me, she dropped her head down into her hands and with a deep gasping breath said the words, "I'm Pregnant" before raising her head to look at me. It sent my mind into an unexpected spiral, as I blankly responded, "You pregnant? How? Since when? Naw, you a lie."

Sierra replied, "NO I AM NOT! I went to the doctor when I was up there because I kept vomiting and couldn't eat anything. At first, they thought that I had a stomach virus, but when it lasted for more than five weeks, the doctor finally asked me, if I had been sexually active within the last few months. After I told them, 'Yeah,' they gave me a pregnancy test and confirmed that I was pregnant."

Completely stunned, I placed my head down into my hands because I couldn't believe this was happening. Lashing out, I said to her, "Naw man, I don't believe you, you lying. You're just trying to find any reason for us to get back together and by telling me you pregnant, you thought this was going to make everything smooth again. You know you messed up in the head Sierra. Like I don't understand you. Why would you even come over here and try to run that bull shit game on me?"

"I AM NOT LYING TO YOU!" she yelled. "Why would you even think that I would even come over here and make up a stupid ass lie about me being pregnant? How dumb and desperate do you think I am?" Sarcastically, I replied, "I don't know. Apparently, really dumb and desperate, since you thought I was going to sit here and let you convince me that you were pregnant, just so that we could get back together."

Raising her voice, she said to me, "Who the hell are you calling dumb? I'm not the one who dropped out of high school because I couldn't man up to my mistakes or who gave up on everything I worked hard for, including the one person who ever gave a shit about me. I'm not lying to you, you jackass. And yes, I did hope that once we had this conversation, you'd be happy about it and maybe we'd be able to figure something out because I love you."

"Well, one; I still think you're lying about being pregnant and two; If you are pregnant, then you need to get an abortion because I don't want nothing to do with you and no baby. You're tripping." But after I said that to her, things escalated quickly, as the angry Sierra replied, "GET AN ABORTION? What in the hell do you mean get an abortion? How dare you tell me that I need to get an abortion, when you the one who laid me down, took off my clothes and got me pregnant? I swear I hate your dumbass. You such an asshole," she screamed, as her eyes pooled with tears.

"Man, you can keep talking about being pregnant all you want. How I know, you ain't go up there and get pregnant by some other dude, and now you want to blame this shit on me? We barely see each other and now all of a sudden you pregnant, man get the hell out here with that bullshit. And tell me, how in the hell you expect us to take care of the baby when neither one of us got a pot to piss in or a window to throw it out. I still can't get a job, cause all these folks doing is looking out for they own people down here. Plus, I don't even have a high school diploma to even apply for a better job. What we supposed to do Sierra, huh?" I replied.

"SHUT THE HELL UP!" she yelled, "I have never cheated on you, even when we were on the worst of terms. You sound like a real jackass right now. You are acting like I don't have parents that will be able to help us take care of this baby. I already have to move back home to finish school at Miami Dade, so I don't see what's the problem. You not being able to get a job, is something that you could've been working on a long time ago if you would've listened to me and started the high school completion program like I told you to. Uh, I swear you just make me want to punch you in your face right now, how sick you make me with the stupid crap you say."

Unconvinced, I said to her, "Man look, one thing about it Sierra. I'll never put my hands on you, so you ain't going to put your hands on me. I don't care how mad you get and besides I'm not trying to hear all that bull crap you talk. My mind is already made up; we ain't having no baby. You been gone all this time and then gon' come back home trying to drop this pregnancy shit on me. You done lost your mind."

"Lost my mind?" she responded. "No, let's not get started on people losing their mind. So, I'ma be the bigger person and act like you never even said that." Clapping her hands together and looking at the ceiling of the car, she regretfully said, "I just find it really funny, how you're going to sit up here and blame me for cheating and lying about being pregnant. When you the main person who is never answering the phone or somehow always busy with their friends when I call you."

Shaking my head because I knew where this conversation was going. I opened the door, got out of the car and walked back to the house. Sitting outside for nearly five minutes, she blew up my phone, attempting to get me to come back outside and talk. But, when she realized that I wasn't going to pick up or get back out, she sped off from in front of the house, causing her tires to squeal and kick up dirt.

CHAPTER 12

A SHADOWS BREATH

THERE WE STAND the darkest entity of the light spectrum. Lacking both character and characteristics, many refer to us as the rectum. Trying to justify the eyes of him who have none but nevertheless, sees more than what is written. Hears more than what is heard, while subconsciously, words become more than just adjectives and verbs. Feelings of unsettled breath rest upon our soul, as the dark energy irreversibly grows, while the moonlight is there to pave a new road. Because by day, the impression of perfection has infected the selection of our direction, inevitably influencing this involuntary discretion. Leaving somber expressions present as we hide in plain sight. In our lonesome, as those that pass nearby herd like cattle, the sight of a mind without a physical presence manifest him to be seen, only and always as a shadow.

Awakening from the slums of Urban America after overstaying my time in the desolate plains underneath the street lights. I could feel the dampness of my pants and the foul smell of the feces that had made its way down my leg. Lying there alone, my soul ached for the emancipation of my self-pity. I found myself battling the illusion of truth vs. reality, as neither had presented itself with clarity.

My muscles felt tender, as I struggled to lift myself from the concrete surface. "What was I doing here?" I asked myself, "How'd I even get here?" As it turns out, while I was hanging out with my boys the day before, we had gotten into a car and began to hotbox it with clouds of marijuana culminated the air. After a few puffs, I began to feel light-headed; my vision grew blurry, my chest started to feel as though the weight of the universe was crashing down upon me.

Holding my hand against my chest as my body laid limp, I cried out, "Aye, y'all boys, I think I'm tripping, but I can barely breathe." One of the guys replied in a joking manner, "Man that's that loud. It'll do it to you," as he laughed it off not taking my words seriously. But to me, I was feeling something completely different, as my head started throbbing, my stomach turned upside down, and my vision slowly decreased with each second passing.

In one last attempt, I weakly reached over into the front seat, asking them to pull over and let down the windows. But to their amusement, what I was going through wasn't as severe as I thought it was. Soon after, I slumped over into one of my boys' lap before falling to the floor of the car. My world had turned dark, and suddenly the loud music playing came to a halt.

My homie sitting in the backseat, taped on the guy's shoulder sitting in the front passenger seat, as he laughs hysterically while saying, "Yo! This mud is knocked out cold. He done passed out back here. He a light weight." But as fell into what felt like a dark void of eternity, I couldn't feel my body and shortly after, the convulsions began. I vigorously rumbled against the back of the passenger seat, as white foam gushed from the sides of my mouth.

Not realizing what was happening, they flipped me over while still laughing, until they eventually saw that my eyes were rolled backward and the veins in my forehead and neck were protruding through my skin. Panicking, my homie in the back seat yelled out, "Yo! Stop the car! Stop the car! I think he's having a seizure."

The tires squealed, as the driver smashed the brake pedal to the floor, leaving behind a small trail of tire markings against the pavement with a small haze of dust lingering behind. Leaning over the seat, the driver frantically ordered them to lift me up and turn me on my side.

As my body slowly stopped twitching, they watched as I began to lay there lifeless. Looking at each other with their eyes exploding widely, one of them said, "Yo, check his pulse man. Make sure he still breathing." But when they felt for a pulse, I had none. Sending them into an immediate panic, as the driver turned around and began to bang his hand on the dashboard.

One of the fellas, said, "Yo, maybe we can take him to the hospital. It ain't nothing but a few minutes away. If we leave now, we can just drop him off at the ER and clear it before anybody see us." Believing the idea wasn't the best option because they were all on probation, the passenger said, "We can't do that bruh. If we do that, they going to see us on the camera and if they catch us they going to try to say we killed him. I ain't trying to go back to jail, so we got to find somewhere else to drop him off that won't lead back to us."

Understanding his logic, they all agreed that it would be best to drop me off somewhere less suspicious. Driving around with a presumed dead person, the car remained as silent as a mouse, until one of the guys said, "Aye, let's go drop him under the bridge by Moore Park. Don't nobody be around there this time of night and if we hurry up, nobody will see us."

Not thinking twice about the suggestion, the driver whipped the car into a fast U-turn and headed towards the new destination. As they pulled up, the driver ordered the other three guys to hurry up and get out. They placed my body on the sidewalk near the underpass of the bridge, before quickly speeding off into the abyss of the night.

Left for dead, my helpless body laid there for hours as the world around me continued to move along without notice. When the afternoon came, I eventually awoke from my detriment with the feeling of sheer agony. The little slice of hope I had left in life was already diminishing, but once I realized what happened to me, it completely vanished. At that point, I knew what I needed to do next to reconcile this feeling of hopelessness.

Heading down the street in my soiled pants, with every step, my soul filled with more determination than ever before. Jogging across a busy main street, I spotted someone who I hadn't talked to in a while. It was my boy Chad. As I caught up to him, I could see that his eyes were bloodshot red and he looked as though he hadn't slept in days.

I called out to him, "Aye yo, Chad. What's up, man? Where you going?" But to no avail, he didn't respond as he continued to walk down the street. Once I got closer to him, I asked, "What's up man, everything been good with you? You look like somebody done pissed you off." Still, he didn't respond to me.

Walking a bit faster, I stood in front of him trying to slow him down, but he continued to walk right through me. I could see that whatever he was focused on, he was determined to get it accomplished. I walked along side of him just in case I needed to back him up, almost forgetting about my pants being soiled.

Continuing to walk alongside him, he abruptly stopped and out of nowhere said, "What are you doing tomorrow for New Year's Eve?" I replied, "I'm supposed to be going over to my grandma Sheryl house, but I don't know if I want to because the ole girl and Gary will probably be over there." Staring at me, he responded, "Cool. How much money do you have on you?"

Searching through my pockets, I noticed that they were empty and realized that my so-called 'homeboys' had taken my money before dumping me on the side of the road. So, I replied, "Shit them Buster took my money. Well, now I don't have nothing on me. Why what's up"? That's when he said, "I need you to get two hundred and fifty dollars by tomorrow. When you do, meet me outside of the pawn shop on Seventh Avenue by 8 o'clock." Confused but trusting Chad, I didn't bother to question his instructions, as I raced home to clean myself up and get the money.

After taking a shower, I woke up the next day ready. As night fall came, I put on all black clothes and began my quest for the two hundred dollars by first asking my aunty Shay. "Hey Aunty," I yelled out as she stood in the kitchen cooking. "You know I don't like asking you for stuff, but I kind of need a favor." Twisting her body around to the right, as she stirred the pot of pasta she was preparing for tomorrow.

"You remember that time I let you hold seventy-five dollars? You think you can give it back to me right now? I got something I need to do, and I'm short like two fifty." Looking at me she said, "I ain't got it right now DJ. I just had to use my friend food stamps card to buy this food." Attempting to plead with her, I stood on the wall near the opening of the kitchen. "Aunty, Please! I really need this money. Can you just stay true to your word and give me back the money I loaned you?" I replied. "DJ, I said I don't have it. I only got money to pay the water bill, but that's about it. Ask me next week when I get paid, and I'll see what I can do."

"What you can do?" I said as I sucked my teeth, "C'mon now Aunty, you told me you were going to give me my money back, and I don't ever ask you for anything. The least you can do is give me back the money, I'm begging you." Dropping the wooden spoon, she was using to stir the pot with, Aunty turned around and asserted, "Who the hell you think you talking to boy? You must've lost your damn mind. I suggest, you go outside and find it before you get your ass slapped."

Realizing that I had made a bad move, I immediately apologized. "Look, Aunty Shay, I'm sorry for talking to you like that, but it's just that, I really need this money to go buy something and the guy said that if I don't come pick it up today, he won't be able to guarantee it'll be there tomorrow. I would've been asked you, but I just made up my mind on buying it yesterday. So, if you can please let me get the money, Aunty, I promise I won't ask you for nothing else ever again."

"I understand it's been tough for you to get a job and all but you going to have to tighten up DJ. I always told you that I wasn't going to be giving you any money, so you lucky you loaned me that money. Look in my purse, and when you open it, you should see a white envelope in there. Take it out, get your seventy-five dollars and leave me alone," she told me.

Relieved that she finally cooperated, I hustled up to her room, scavenged through her purse until I found that white envelope and snagged out the seventy-five dollars. As soon as I grabbed it, I hurried out of the door. I headed to the pawn shop, where Chad told me to meet him. I managed to come up with all of the money because I used some of the cash that I had stashed in one of my old shoe boxes. When I got there, I saw him standing out front wearing all black, just as was.

When I got closer, he asked vehemently, "You got the rest of the money?" Reassuring him, I said, "Yeah, as I pulled the cash out of my jacket pocket and handed it over to him. With the rest of the money in his hand, he then turned around and walked into the pawn shop. Coming back out a few moments later, he asked, "What time does the next Metrorail come?" I replied, "Like 9:30 pm, why?" He then began to walk towards a nearby bus stop before stopping and saying, "You coming or what?"

I was confused by Chad's new attitude because I couldn't figure out what would cause him to act so stealth like and suspicious. To be honest, it reminded me of myself a bit, which was weird. But as we walked to the bus stop, we both remained silent before getting on a bus that led us to the North Dade Metrorail Station.

With no security around, we hopped the fence of the Metrorail Station and ran up the stairs that lead to the tracks. The strange energy circulated throughout the night, as we both stared out the window on the bumpy train ride. Reaching our destination in Coconut Grove, we stepped off the train and walked towards the busy main street. The night was full of life, as cars flew by and the sound of music resonated with the distinction of the city's magical aura.

The two of us headed down a dark alleyway, where we spotted a poorly lit parking lot. Seeing an older model Nissan, we decided that it was the car we were going to take. Sprinting over to the car, we made sure that we stayed low so that no one would be able to spot us.

Popping the lock on the car, we hopped in and hotwired the car. The crazy thing was that, all the other times I had been up to no good, I would always feel a sense of impending doom. But tonight, I felt a captivating sensation of accomplishment and thrill. Taking the car, we drove around the entire night before parking and falling asleep in the car.

It was New Year's Eve, and the alarming sound of neighborhood roosters in Little Havana woke us from our deep sleep. With our stomachs growling, we made a quick stop at a fast food restaurant to grab something to eat. The silence persisted between us, but the energy flowed along the spectrum of an unspoken sense of peace.

The evening was approaching, so I asked if it was okay for us to stop by to see Sierra. I knew that she and I had ended on bad terms, but I just wanted to express my deepest sympathy and abundance of appreciation I had for her. But the trip was a complete waste, as she threatened to call the police on me if I didn't leave her house, while her mom came to the door screaming with a bat in her hand.

My mistakes had finally caught up with me. I was left with only one person that could understand everything I was going through, but it didn't matter much because for some reason although Chad was present, his mind appeared to be somewhere else. I guess, whatever he had on his mind, he couldn't remove it. At times, I would catch him, just staring out the window into nowhere land.

As the sun was beginning to set and the moon shined brightly. We rolled around in the stolen car for a bit, before eventually pulling up to my old stomping grounds at my grandma Sheryl's apartment. She was still living in the same ole two-bedroom apartment on the second floor.

Opening the door of the car, I briefly paused before heading up the stairs, gazing upon the spot where Jaleel had been killed. Walking up to the door, I threw my hoodie over my head and knocked on the door. "Who is it?" A voice from inside the apartment had shouted before a figure walked towards the door. When they got closer, I could see that it was my mama.

We locked eyes, and instantly my heart began to palpitate because I didn't know what to expect from her. She then sucked her teeth, unlocked the bottom lock and headed back to her seat on the couch. When I walked in, I saw my little brother laying on the floor sleep. I wanted to pick him up to kiss him on the forehead, but I left him alone to avoid having to hear my mama's mouth.

The smell of freshly baked cornbread, BBQ beef ribs and chicken flooded the entire house. Walking in, I said, "Hey," to my grandma Sheryl but she just waved at me with the face of disappointment. My uncle Sherman was sitting at the small dining room table wedged between the sofa and kitchen.

"Hey, hey nephew," he stuttered, "Long time no see," he said while reaching out to shake my hand. Moments later, I heard the toilet flush and saw Aunty Shay walking out of the bathroom. "What's up nephew," she said, "Did you ever go get what you needed to get yesterday?" Nodding my head and softly speaking, I responded, "Yeah, I went and got it."

That's when she asked me, "You hungry? It's a whole lot of food over there, fix you a plate. I responded, "Naw, that's alright Aunty. I'll be good." Not fond of my response, she said, "Boy, if you don't get behind up and go eat now cause when everybody else gets over here I don't want to hear you talking about, 'All the food gone.'"

She then handed me a plastic plate and began to fill it up with food. Sitting at the table eating, I watched my little brother as he laid there sleeping peacefully. I imagined all the things that he would be dreaming of and even what he will grow up to be like. I just hoped that whatever it was, he didn't grow up to be anything like me.

Glancing over at my mother, I could see that she was still the same ole her. Her eyes didn't have the same glow as they used to have when I was a kid but her skin was still as vibrant as the sun. Once I finished eating, I threw the remaining bones on my plate into the trash and announced to everyone that I was leaving.

My aunty said, "Well dang. You weren't over here for more than thirty minutes, and you're already leaving? What you leaving so early for?" Not able to give her a clear answer, I replied, "I got to go do something. Somebody waiting for me downstairs." She then said to me, "Well tell them to come up here then. They can get a plate and eat with us. Ain't nobody gon' bite them."

"Naw Aunty, It's straight. We just got to go, so don't worry about it."

"I guess," she replied, "Well, just make sure that you call me ahead of time if you plan on coming home tonight," Reticently, I responded, "Yeah, I got you, Aunty," before standing up to give her a hug. But as she tried to step back to sit down, I continued to hold her tightly.

She leaned her head back and in a worried voice said to me, "Nephew, you okay? Something wrong with you? With no reply, I just held onto her, as tears began to bubble in my eyes. "Nephew, are you sure you okay? she asked, before pulling my arms from around her and grabbing onto my face while looking me in the eyes.

Wiping my eyes clear of tears, I responded, "Yeah, I'm good Aunty. My bad, I just wanted to show you how much I loved you, that's all."

"Aww," she replied, before reaching in to hug me for a second time.

Slowly backing away from her, I said, "Bye Aunty," as I headed towards the front door. Noticing that my little brother was starting to move, I kneeled next to him and began to rub his soft little curly haired head. He was my hope for life, and I knew that he was going to bring my mama a lot more joy in this world than I ever had. Standing up, I looked over at my mom and said, "Ma!"

Remaining focused on the TV, she didn't even blink, as she deliberately ignored me. To show her that I still had love for her, I leaned over and tried to kiss her on the cheek, but she moved her face out of the way and gave me the stare of "death." Backing away, my words trembled, as I said to her, "I love you Ma," while tears began to fill my eyes once again. In that very moment, it sealed the deal for me. All the pain, the disappointment, the misery, everything bad that I had ever felt in this world, was suddenly amplified.

Running down the staircase, I hurried back to the car before bursting in a well of tears. "Just drive!" I said, signaling Chad to pull off from in front of the apartment. Shifting the car into drive, we slowly drove away. Continuing to cry during the heat of the night, the rain droplets drifting down the windshield sparkled, as the dull incandescent streets light glared upon us.

Driving around for thirty minutes, we finally came to rest in an open lot near some railroad tracks. With the air conditioning blowing, condensation quickly began to fog the windows, and the rain continued to pour down relentlessly. Closing my eyes, I leaned my head against the window and cried, trying to understand what have I done to deserve this much pain in my life.

There's no way that anyone should have to go through this much pain in life for no reason at all. Slowly opening my eyes to check on Chad, I grew uneasy when I saw that he was sitting in the driver's seat with a gun laying on his lap. "Chad, what's up? What you got a gun for, bruh?" I asked in a panic.

Twirling the gun in his hands, tears began to drop from his face as he lifted his head towards the ceiling of the car, took a deep gulp and said to me with his voice cracking, "I'm just so freaking tired of hurting man. It's like, everything thing that I try to do in life is always wrong. I can never seem to make myself or anybody else around me happy.

"My family doesn't care about me, my girl doesn't want me no more, I almost died yesterday, and still nobody gives a shit or cares about the pain I go through man. It's like everybody else is always expecting me to accept shit and just get over everything, but I can't man. I can't take it no more man; I just can't."

"Chad! Bruh! I know that this life we've been giving is tough, but we can't allow the pressure of it, to force us into giving up. We got to fight. I remember this one time when Sierra asked me if I cared about living or dying? When she asked me that, I'll be honest; I couldn't tell the two apart because it seemed like my whole life I've been drowning in deep waters, just barely keeping my head afloat to survive.

"But I can tell you right now, that I realized one important thing, which is; We only get one life to live bruh. So, what we choose to do with it, that's something we have to live with. My whole life I've been mad at the entire world. I hated it for taking my dad away who never got the chance to teach me how to be a man, for taking away my little cousin that never got the opportunity to grow up and reach his potential, to dealing with Gary and my mama never taking my side.

"But I also realized that it wasn't always bad either. If it wasn't for certain people coming into my life at times when I was down, I don't know if I would even be here right now. So, sometimes we got to take the good with the bad and look forward to all the great things we have yet to see. So, bruh - trust me when I tell you things will get better. You a survivor. So, just give me the gun and let me hold it for you," I said as I reached over to take the gun away from him.

Snatching his hands away, he moved the gun towards his head and began to cry hysterically. "Bruh, No! I hear you, but I just can't do this shit anymore. I don't want to have to wake up and worry about if someone is going to catch me slipping in the streets, if I'm going to have to go through the pain of watching another loved one die or if anybody in this world is ever going to give a shit about me.

"I just can't do it, DJ, I just can't do this shit no more he said," as I watched his hyperventilating chest dramatically expand in & out and without any warning. He looked over at me with his glossy eyes, of a somber soul in despair, and said the words, "I'm sorry," before pulling the trigger of the gun.

POW!

As the sound of the loud gunshot echoed through the car, my ears began to ring, and my vision began to get blurry, as I attempted to hold myself together from the sight of blood spattered all over the car window. Then suddenly, I fell unconscious.

The next evening, a family was bringing in their New Year's with a small family celebration, when a loud banging sound was heard coming from the front door.

"Who is it?" A woman asked as she walked towards the door. To her surprise, it was a man dressed in a white shirt with a black tie.

"Hello ma'am, my name is Detective Aaron Wilson with the City of Miami Police Department. Do you happen to know if anyone by the name of Brianna Walters or someone that goes by the nickname 'Red,' currently resides at this address? I'd like to ask her a few questions, regarding a case I am currently investigating."

"Yes, my name is Brianna Walters, and they call me Red. What you need to talk to me for?" The detective calmly replied, "Ma'am if it's okay, would you mind stepping outside, so that I can briefly ask you a few questions?" Holding a baby boy on the side of her waist, she reluctantly opened the door and said, "Sure, why not."

Detective Wilson then opened a manila folder that had a copy of an Identification Card and asked, "Does the individual, Chadwick Mills, currently reside at this address? With a bitter tone, she replied, "No he doesn't, but that's my son. Why what his dumbass done got himself into now? Whatever his dumbass as did, if y'all catch him. Keep him."

The detective lowered his head and proceeded with saying, "Ma'am, I'm sorry, but I regret to inform you that, about a few hours ago we were contacted about a stolen vehicle being spotted in an empty lot near train tracks. When our patrol officers got to the scene, they found the body of your son in the stolen car. Our report shows that your kid was killed by what seems to be a self-inflicted gunshot wound to the head."

Quickly snatching the folder out of the detective's hand, her heart raced as he said, "What!? No! Where in the hell is my son? Naw, y'all got the wrong person cause he was just here last night, so that's not my child body y'all got. I'm sorry but Chad might act like he crazy but he ain't that stupid."

"Well, I'm sorry ma'am, but this is the identification card that we found on the body of the victim and what you just told me, matches what out medical examiner stated. Somehow, from the time he left here to approximately 3:30 am this incident occurred." Hearing those devastating words, the woman's knees suddenly buckled beneath her, sending her sliding down the frame of the door before bursting in a howl of screams.

Rapidly, two other women came running to the door to see what was going on, as Chad's mother laid in the doorway bursting in tears. Approaching the door, the sister of the woman walked up and said, "Bri, get up! What are you crying for? What's wrong with you?" But unresponsive and filled with the crushing sensation of grief, the woman Bri, continued to sob profusely.

Looking over at the officer with fury in her eyes, the woman then said to the officer, "What in the hell did you, say to my sister? Why in the hell in is she crying?" Detective Wilson cautiously replied, "Ma'am, please. I want you to calm down and listen to me for a second," while calmly backing away with his hands in the air. "What did you say to her, goddammit? She is my goddamn sister; my name is Shay. So, can you please tell me what's going on?" the woman screamed.

"Ma'am, I'm sorry to bring you this unfortunate news, but it seems as though we've identified her son, nineteen-year-old, Chadwick Mills, as a victim of a possible suicide incident. His body was found in a stolen car, located near an empty lot just north of Liberty City not too long ago, with a single gunshot wound to the head." But as he continued to talk, the woman's eyes grew larger, and her mouth dropped to the floor as she held her chest, while breathing slowly.

The chaos of screaming from Chads' distraught mother, along with a now crying baby, echoed throughout the building. Sending people running out of their apartments and spewing onto the street to be nosey. Attempting to comfort Chad's devastated mom, the mother of the two women prayed and recited Bible verses, while fanning an old magazine over the woman Bri. Rocking back and forth, as she stared off into the emptiness of space, the detective came back into the house and handed the woman Shay a piece of paper. He said that it was a written note they'd recovered from the pants pocket of Chad.

ACKNOWLEDGEMENTS

Living in a world, where pain is anchored by the individual experiences that we go through. I believe that we often become victims to our subconscious. We allow the world to dictate our perspectives of success and define the quality of love that we emit to one another. Self-hatred is not only an issue that young African Americans face but an issue that is found throughout the world, as we all try to embrace the high standards placed upon us by those that can't relate to our day to day struggles.

To shed light on the various experiences of growing up in an environment that is often more traumatic than it is peaceful. I would like to pay tribute to all my close friends and loved ones that I too have lost in this battle of existence we call life. To Brandon Mills and Derrick "Termite" Gloster, who lives were taken way too soon, I express my deepest sympathy, as I was proud to call you both my brothers.

To the young boy, King Carter, who was also taken away at the precious age of six years old, your life will forever be cherished. But to my cousin Daniel Coleman, who battled the discomfort of a mental health condition that would eventually cause you to expedite your ascendance towards realm of eternal life, this book is in your honor.

I would also like to take the time out to thank my fraternity brothers, Rossenel Laguerre & Kevin Ho-Yen for staying on top of me day, in and day out, so that I would get this book accomplished. May the true spirit of brotherly love forever live through your hearts and thank you for your diligent encouragement. It also wouldn't be right, if I didn't mention the entire Chapter of the Usual Suspects, much love to all of my brothers.

I am forever grateful for my family and those that have supported me consistently throughout my journey in life. A special thanks to Anthony Lindsey Jr, Emanuel Peterson Jr., Jarvis Mangham, Joshua Corbitt, Kush Carmichael, Mondaryll Latrez and Winston Bishop.

Also, A very dear and extra special "Thank You" to Mrs. Indra Campbell & Fakaira Gabriel for reading this book in manuscript form and playing a huge role in helping me edit this book to the best of your ability. Thank You, for assisting me in bringing my vison to life.

Resources for Diagnosing & Seeking Assistance for Mental Health

Remember, never be afraid to seek professional care as the resources provided are solely listed as suggestions.

- Drug & Alcohol Treatment Hotline
  1-800-662-4359
- National Suicide Prevention Lifeline
  1-800-273-8255
- National Alliance on Mental Illness (NAMI) L
  1-800-950-6264
- Sexual Abuse – Stop It Now! Hotline
  1-800-773-8368
- To find information and access to services in your local areas, visit:

  www.MentalHealth.gov

- NAMI: National Alliance of Mental Health Illness
  www.nami.org

- U.S. Department of Human and Human Health Services: Office of Minority Health
  https://minorityhealth.hhs.gov

- What is Mental Illness – What are Signs
  www.mentalhealthamerica.net/recognizing-warnigs-signs

- Tips to Manage Anxiety and Stress: Anxiety and Depression Association of America
  https://www.adaa.org/tips-manage-anxiety-and-stress

Made in the USA
Columbia, SC
15 December 2017